Days of Unease

Preston Ford

Published by A Thousand Candles Press, 2024.

© Copyright 2024 by Preston Ford

All rights reserved. This is a work of fiction. Names, characters, places, and events are either products of the author's imagination or are used fictitiously. Any resemblance to actual persons, living or dead, is coincidental. No part of this book may be used or reproduced in any manner whatsoever without written permission except in the case of brief quotations embodied in critical articles or reviews.

First paperback edition October 2024

Published by A Thousand Candles Press, LLC

www.prestonfordwrites.com

For my Mother...

The Skeptic's Paradox – those who wish most fervently to see supernatural events will be least able to accept those events should they occur.

> **Real** – "[That which has] objective independent existence; not artificial, fraudulent, or illusory: Genuine." – Merriam-Webster

---

Lights in the sky. Sounds in the night.
What is happening...?

Is there a way we can know for certain that a thing is actual? Can we know that it has corporeal substance and is not the creation of a tired mind or a tortured spirit? Can we know beyond doubt that the things we see, hear and feel are occurring in fact? After thousands of years of searching and pondering, humanity still cannot answer these questions with certainty. Is there another side to the universe we live in, a side that only some of us experience?

Some of us—those who are lucky—might never find out.

I.
Awaiting...

(First published in *7th Circle Pyrite: A Literary Journal Celebrating Worlds Beyond*, Issue 6, September 2024)

Dear Katz,

It's been a month and a half, and I've been trying to find a way to tell you how I'm feeling and what I've finally decided to do. You know me. You know I can be a little compulsive in my decision making, even with the serious stuff. I know I sometimes jump first and then look. I promise you I'm not gonna do that this time. You're not going to like what I have to say, but it's been damn near impossible for me to think about anything besides "the discovery" since they put that girl on the news a year ago.

Did you think we would live to see this? For real though. Harvard, MIT, *and* Columbia are all opening departments of Parapsychology in the Fall. Imagine that. How many thousands of years have people been swearing that ghosts and spirits and such are real? And for how many centuries have people like me and the people who run Harvard and MIT been laughing at those other people? But now we know. If that girl in that cemetery hadn't been crazy enough to run toward that thing when she saw it, if she hadn't been...I don't know the right word for it...*caught up* enough to keep filming the thing, how many more lifetimes would have passed without us knowing for sure that those things are out there? I was reading an article in the Wall Street Journal a few days ago, and how they summed it up is one of the best ways I've heard.

I know you don't read the Journal so if you'll forgive the long quote, it said:

"*Graveyard Ghost* is the name of the Pulitzer Prize-winning image that Time Magazine took from the video and used on the cover of that week's issue. It is history's first clearly discernible, fully vetted and corroborated photographic record of an entity whose existence cannot be explained by the laws of physics. *Graveyard Ghost* is to believers in the supernatural what the Rosetta Stone was to scholars of the ancient world. Or more aptly, it is what the hominid skeleton Lucy was to paleontologists. It is the missing link that bridges the divide between modern science and the world that could not be touched (or recorded) until now..."

"The viral video from that evening has been seen more times than any recorded footage in history. It has been studied, analyzed, examined and dissected by more governments, more universities, more corporations, think-tanks, and individuals than any other human artifact. Consider that between 1611 and 2020, more than three billion humans worldwide had read some portion of the King James Bible. The Video...surpassed three billion views in six and a half weeks... [it was seen in] every country, on every continent on Earth (including Antarctica) and viewed by humans no longer on the earth (astronauts aboard the International Space Station). It is the subject of a staggering number of journal articles, doctoral theses, books, blogs, documentaries, and now, major motion pictures. The number of views on YouTube alone is unprecedented: four-point-five billion and counting—more than anything uploaded since the site's inception..."

Every time I watch the video, a part of me still wants to believe it's a fake, but if the thing didn't go away, if the thing is still there *to this day,* how can a person not believe it? If Harvard and MIT say the thing is real, that's good enough for me.

But that's what scares me. And fascinates me. If ghosts are real, can't angels and demons also be real? I know. I know. I do still keep up with Scientific American. I know you're going to point to the same thing my colleagues point to. Quote:

"The existence of a heretofore hidden reality, where entities not understood by science are now known to abide, does not guarantee the existence of gods or demons..." blah blah blah. But Katz, think about it. We believe in science because its tenants are testable, falsifiable. And when we learn new information, we adjust our thinking. For centuries we pushed back against claims of the paranormal because there was no objective, verifiable evidence to support them. Now we have the video of this thing, standing in a graveyard watching a funeral, and it's not some grainy Bigfoot video. It's not blurry and out of focus, and half the universities (and damn near every government) on earth has verified that the picture is real, that the damn thing is there! And we have no idea what it's made of or how it's even there in the first place. It's so funny listening to the conspiracy nuts... Yeah, half the people on the fucking planet want to fool somebody's uncle. Jesus Christ. And then the religious people going back and forth: is it from God? Is it evil? I get so tired of it sometimes, but at the end of the day, I'm like everybody else; I can't stop thinking about it.

At this point, you and I are the only people I know who don't swear they've been seeing ghosts all their lives. I still haven't seen one. Have you seen one yet? Why do you think that is? Is it because we don't crave attention enough to lie for it? Or because we don't hop on the bandwagon and co-sign every new trend that pops up? I get so sick of people talking to empty seats on the subway and swearing it's George Washington or Martin Luther King. Personally, I believe the vast majority of people still don't see them, no matter how much they lie, and I still think anybody who makes a living from claiming to talk to them is full of shit. And isn't it crazy that since the start of the Industrial Revolution, people have complained about how light keeps our brains from truly resting at night, but now most people make sure some lights are *on* before they get in the bed and go to sleep? The world has changed so much, and I just can't get my head around it.

The reason I'm writing, like I said, is to let you know I've been thinking long and hard about something and I've made a decision. You know how those of us who don't believe in UFOs are the ones who are the most eager to see one? Can you imagine how satisfying it would be to touch an actual skin sample? Or see just the taillight of a flying saucer? To see one scrambled text message from an extraterrestrial intelligence? I guess that's *why* we're the biggest skeptics. We want it more than most people can imagine. I remember how you laughed when I signed up to join the crew for that billionaire asshole's Mars colony project. I knew I wouldn't be picked, but I wanted to go so badly and see what was out there. I think you were able to laugh because you also knew I didn't have a chance. It wasn't even clear that the guy was serious, and I didn't even have a degree yet. You knew there wasn't any *real* danger I'd wind up sitting in a space capsule headed across the solar system. I suppose I knew it too, but I wanted—I *needed*—to know. I *needed* to know what was out there, and so I signed up. Now this thing...this thing in the graveyard and humanity suddenly finding itself at this crossroads, on the edge of this whole new age of discovery. It won't leave me alone.

I hope this doesn't frighten you or creep you out. I just don't want you to find out from the authorities. Next week, I'll see my thirtieth birthday. My doctor says a guy like me, if he takes care of himself, can expect to live for 73 years or more.

That means I could be hanging around for four more decades, give or take, wondering what's down that other road. I guess the odds are I *will* see a ghost or two in the next forty years. Just because they aren't showing themselves to me now doesn't mean they never will. But Katz, I can't wait forty years to find out what's out there. I mean, now we *know* there's a whole other plane of existence. And not that I'm qualified to argue with Scientific American, but what if there are gods? What if all the things we were told aren't real really are? What if, when we die, we just change but don't end? I wonder if my mom and dad know what my life has been like. I wonder if they'll know when I'm coming. I wonder if I can find them...

Do you remember the time we were in Spain, and you drew a heart on the bathroom mirror while I was in the shower? It was right after things started going sideways with us, and we were trying to get back on track. When you drew that heart on the mirror, something that small and simple, it let me know your heart was still in it, and we could find our way back to being in love like we had been. I never told you, but I almost cried when I saw it. I was so relieved to find out everything wasn't lost. Well, we did try. We took our teacups, and we tried as hard as we could to dip out that ocean, but, in time, the tide was just too much for us. You can see from this tome I'm sending you, though, that you still are a big part of me. That's why I wanted to tell you myself what's ahead for me. I have to go and find out. If I'm wrong, I'll never know it. But if I'm right...If I'm right Katz, I can't wait to see what's on that other side. I can't imagine how things work over there. Is it a matter of choice where one goes, who one sees? What role does free will play? What role does chance play? I don't know, but whatever the rules are, I'll try to make a heart on the mirror for you. If you see one, you'll know it's me reaching out. You are not a fearful person, and so I imagine it won't frighten you if you already know it might be coming. I just know that I'll want you to know that I'm alright and that I'll never stop thinking about you no matter where I am or what state I'm in.

The most valuable things I own are my car and the money in my accounts. The car's not new but it's still in great shape, so it'll bring a nice piece of change if you decide not to keep it. I've donated most of my clothes and a whole lot of other stuff to the homeless shelter and the thrift store across town. What's left is mostly books and pictures. I'm sure you'll get a call, but don't worry about any of that stuff. I'll put the account numbers at the end of this page.

Don't be scared, Katz. I'm not scared. I'm almost excited. I'm sorry we couldn't fix things, but maybe it was for the best all along. Maybe something bigger than us knew this was coming one day. Who would have imagined that the start of the 21st century, the age of the internet and space tourism, would be the time we would finally have definitive proof that ghosts are real? Anything is possible now. And it's time for me to see it for myself.

I wish you peace and happiness Katz.

Don't forget me.

II.
The End

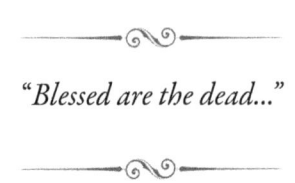

"Blessed are the dead..."

"Professor Todd?"

A soft hand shakes me, calling me back from the long nightmare that has held me captive for what feels like days. I sit up, startled, and look around at the walls of my office. A colorful abstract artwork woven from strands of plant fiber and given to me by an African diplomat hangs reassuringly on the wall above the filing cabinets.

The woman is tall and wears glasses. She is my teaching assistant. She hands me a manila folder stuffed with carefully typed essays and her grade recommendations for each. I take the folder and fumble with my own glasses which are askew on my forehead. She gives me a quasi-sympathetic look, one that wavers between irritation and pity.

"You really ought to take a day off and just rest," she says. Her tone, along with the brown spots on her hands and the gray visible at her temples make her seem more like my mother than a graduate student marking time until the end of the semester.

She continues to speak as I look over the papers.

"You can't make that deadline if you're laid up in a hospital."

I have almost finished my first work of fiction, and my editor is pushing me to get it done so that it can be in stores before the end of the year. My other books were well received. Now, I am trying something larger, something riskier and more demanding. The preliminary feedback has been so encouraging that she (my editor) feels certain it will clinch an award in the coming spring if it can be gotten out in time to compete with this year's crop of new fiction.

I am less concerned with the idea of winning something than with the desire to have the whole thing finished so that I can concentrate on my class load. My contract says nothing about time off to write novels. One could even argue that I am cheating the university and my students, giving them less than their money's worth when I show up late to class, my brain fuzzy, and my lessons only half prepared.

She continues to chastise me as I look through the essays and I think 'Oh well.' A couple more months and all will be back to normal. No one will have the slightest cause to complain—not my editor, not my assistant, not my students, not the university. No one.

"Everyone else is gone," she says.

She resists adding "can I go now?" but her tone makes it clear she does not wish to wake me up again. She has high school-aged children, but I have no doubt she would rather be at home with them than here with me.

"Why don't you call it a night?" I say to her.

The campus is dark and the night warm. The grounds and the dormitories are never completely still, but I can see no cars moving on the street outside my first-floor office window. Water droplets dot the lower half of the windowpane; the lawn sprinklers have emerged from the ground to moisten the parched flowerbeds and the grass, which will soon need cutting.

"Shall I walk you to your car?" I ask.

"That's okay," she says hurriedly, "thanks. I'll call for an escort. Goodnight."

There is fumbling in the outer office and then the click of her heels as she disappears down the hall.

It's nine o'clock, but I press on. I will stop in a little while and go over the notes for my eight-a.m. class. My assistant is right, of course, but there is no rest for the weary.

Or is it the wicked?

Soon there are no sounds at all except the clacking of keys and the occasional buzz of the hard drive. It would feel so good to lay my head down and steal a few minutes of sleep, but I still have miles to go before I can justify sleeping.

Soon, I remind myself. Soon this will all be over.

As I write, my left eye starts to sting, telling me it has gone from slightly red to completely bloodshot. Tomorrow, everyone who sees me will ask if I have pinkeye, or if my allergies are acting up; no one ever thinks of sleep deprivation.

I let go of the keyboard and sink into the soft leather of the chair, closing both eyes. Warmth and numbness wash over me in waves.

Miles to go before I sleep…

The rain woke me up. A light sprinkling at first, it quickly turned into a violent downpour with wind and water rattling the windows like poltergeists trying to force their way in.

I sat up and stretched. It didn't feel like I had fallen asleep; I'd only closed my eyes for a minute. But in that brief time, someone had crept into the office and switched off the overhead light.

I was annoyed.

Some Freshman still clinging to adolescence was probably standing on the other side of the door, waiting to jump at me when I got up to turn the light back on.

I sighed.

The outer office was empty and dark but for the orange glow of lights from the parking lot showing through the blinds. I went to the door and looked down the long hallway that led to the other offices. Voices and the glow of a television set emanated from a room farther down.

I left my office and went toward the light, passing as I did a pair of French doors that opened onto a small courtyard. Rain lashed against the panes with incredible energy, as if a firehose had been aimed at the glass. I paused and moved the thin curtain aside to look out. The wind had bent a row of dogwood saplings to better than forty-five-degree angles. All would be shorn of their leaves and maybe even uprooted by the time the storm ended.

Turning back toward the office where the blue light was, I went to the door and looked in. A handful of people were listening in silence to a news bulletin. I listened for a moment then turned and walked back to the French doors. I moved the curtain aside again, and this time I saw that the rain had stopped. As suddenly and unexpectedly as it had come, the powerful storm had vanished. I opened one of the doors and looked out.

The air was still.

I stepped outside and looked down at the walkway. The concrete was jaundice-yellow in the light of the gas lamps and showed no sign of the drenching it had undergone just moments ago. I stooped to touch it and, indeed, it was completely dry. I went to the edge of the walkway, reached down and clutched a handful of blades of grass.

They were dry.

I looked up at the sky.

In the darkness above me, three stars glittered with crimson malevolence. I gazed at them, and my eyes drew the lines that formed a triangular constellation, one that I, an avid stargazer, had never seen. High in the west, they stared back at me like the eyes of an immense beast while clouds black as the soot from a coal fire floated past and obscured their light.

I went back inside and closed the doors behind me.

There were more people milling about now, and more had crowded into the room with the television. I stuck my head in and listened while a white-haired commentator in a dark blue suit calmly spoke to three others about the collapse of the U.S.-China peace talks.

"The White House confirmed just minutes ago..."

Two American aircraft carrier battle groups had taken up positions in the Philippine Sea off the coast of Taiwan. A third was on its way. The tough-talking American President, a swaggering imbecile oblivious to his own shortcomings, had ordered the fleet to deploy and provide a firewall in case the Chinese decided to move against the island nation. In response, the Chinese had massed an entire amphibious army in the southern Fujian province just across the Taiwan Strait.

They called it a defensive force, but a single word from Beijing and it would become an invasion force comparable to those put ashore at Normandy and Okinawa at the end of World War II. Now, each side was faced with backing up its tough rhetoric or abandoning the island to its adversary for all the foreseeable future.

I thought of the Cold War, the decades-long standoff between the US and the USSR, and I marveled at how it had already become the stuff of abstract history. In less than half a lifetime, the world had relaxed from hair-trigger nuclear readiness only to return to it later when it seemed climate change was the most serious problem on earth. Two nations were again poised to destroy themselves and the entire world in an argument over land that belonged to neither.

How had we come back to this?

Two things and two things only were certain: there was no place to hide, and once either side pushed the button, it would all be over very quickly. Unless cooler heads—or a higher power—prevailed, the approaching midnight might well be the world's last.

Someone got up quietly and left the room; everyone else continued to listen. Even more people had crowded into the doorway behind me. I turned and picked my way through the press of bodies, intending to go back to my office and continue working.

There were two men in the hallway outside my office. They wore dark business suits even at this late hour. It did not register right away that they might be there to see me, but they stopped me as I tried to enter and asked me to identify myself.

I told them who I was and then asked them if they wouldn't mind doing the same. They followed me inside.

One of the men took a seat across from my desk and the other stopped and stood by the door.

Outside my office window, the rain had started again.

The man who had sat down began talking, telling me not who they were but why they were there, and the things he said made me wonder if he were insane. He talked without stopping for almost twenty minutes, not answering my questions but hurrying to finish some long-winded explanation of something, and when he fell silent, I gazed at him dumbfounded while the rain beat against the window behind me.

My mother, this man wanted me to understand, was alive again.

His partner stepped forward and placed a leather case on the other chair and opened it. He drew out a thick gray binder and offered it to me as his partner watched.

It was a hospital chart.

I opened it, and there at the very front was the death certificate bearing her name, the same one I had seen twelve years ago. The succeeding pages—radiology reports, progress notes, lab results—recounted in detail the slow progression of her cancer. Flipping through them, I relived in those few moments the long months of her decline.

No ventilator for her, I recalled. No serene crossing. She had suffered as though God himself held a grudge against her, and when the end was near, I would have pulled the plug without hesitation for my own sake as much as for hers had there been a plug to pull. Now, miraculously (or tragically) I was being told that a woman whom I watched die twelve years earlier was alive.

It would have been easier to believe I'd been lost for years in a stress-induced hallucination. I could have believed I was drugged out of my mind at that very moment and imagining all of this. But they weren't telling me I was delirious and seeing things: they were telling me she had died...and she had recovered.

I was there when she became so weak she could hardly gasp for breath, when she could no longer see. Her eyes had been fine, but she reached a point where she could no longer make out who I was even though my face hovered inches from hers or was pressed against it. I had begged them to give her morphine when she was no longer able to ask for it herself but was clearly racked with pain. I had prayed that she would die. I had asked God to let me die in her place because I deserved it and she did not. I had even thought of placing the pillow over her face, but I couldn't because I thought even that might hurt her, and I only wanted her pain to stop. Now, two mysterious individuals dressed like characters from a science fiction movie were telling me not that she had survived her illness, but that she had *died*—suffered full clinical and brain death—and then, days later, she had been revived.

"The hell is wrong with you people?" I said to him, my voice grating in my throat. "What's the matter with you? Do you think this is funny?"

I am not a large man but spurred by the fury and the disgust I felt at that moment, I could have thrown that desk aside like a plastic serving tray and beat the shit out of both these men.

"Get the fuck out of my office. Get the fuck out, before I—"

He raised one hand, surrendering. With the other, he took an iPad from the briefcase and laid it on the desk in front of me. The video had been shot at an awkward angle, but there was no mistaking what it showed.

Her salt-and-pepper hair was completely white now. Her eyes were closed, and a breathing mask covered her mouth and nose. An attendant sat in a chair next to the bed and gazed at a television set on which I could see the President standing behind the podium in the White House Briefing Room. Plastered across the bottom of the screen were the words: "Tensions Increase in the Taiwan Strait."

I fell backward in my chair.

They had told me how, supposedly, and they had anticipated my confusion and incredulity; I needed to ask and keep asking. But they could not have anticipated the anguish that hit me when I watched the video. The man who had handed me the chart spoke.

They could only tell me so much, he said. In the murky depths where arcane research and national security crossed paths, someone—or *some ones*—had appropriated fourteen newly deceased bodies from hospitals in the city where she had died. Each had expired less than twenty-four hours before being seized. Spirited away to a place he would not name, they were experimented upon, injected with something, pumped full of something else. The cellular decomposition had slowed drastically in all fourteen; in three, it had stopped altogether. Twelve years later, those three were in and out of comas and showed signs of Alzheimer's, but all three were alive and able to breathe on their own.

She was one of them.

I got up, shaking, and walked out of the room, clutching the iPad like a live electrical wire. I wanted to go to this place and see this for myself; I had to see if this were real, even though I knew it could not be.

Twelve years. Twelve years of unnatural sleep.

These men were lying. Or I was dreaming.

Either way, this was insane. A horrible, tasteless prank perhaps. Maybe all of the above. Whose ashes had I scattered on the Potomac River if not my mother's?

One of the men followed me to the outer office. He told me that the decision to make the research public had come from very high up in the government. The families would be well compensated (as if money could right the outrage of what they claimed to have done), but first we had to be told.

The rain stopped again.

I found myself back at the French doors, opening them against damp air this time, seeing the grass glisten in the light of passing cars. There was movement all over the campus now, people loading into cars and driving away.

Overhead, the three stars that I had seen earlier, the three red eyes, seemed brighter. Looking at them reminded me of the newscast, and I noticed that despite movement everywhere there was no excitement or panic.

Everyone on earth knew the seriousness of the situation the two superpowers had created. After hearing that the last attempt to reach an agreement had failed, I expected to feel the full weight of doom pressing down on the world and to see people acting accordingly. Were failed peace talks not the cue for the survivalist rituals to begin? This was the time when people headed for the hills in movies, when the cities began to burn, and the breakdown of law and order got underway. I had kept this military crisis at the back of my mind, in denial perhaps, for days, yet a part of me had all along believed that if the talks ran into trouble, there would be chaos in the streets. As I struggled to make sense of all that I had seen and heard in the last hour, I noted that there were no prayer vigils, no hysterics among the growing numbers emerging from the buildings. All over the campus, students stood in groups and talked quietly. Others in loose bands had started toward the highway on foot. One student whom I knew well, a young man who had confided in me on occasion, stood nearby with his arm around an incredible young woman whom he had not had the courage to speak to just days ago. The two of them had their eyes fastened on the heavens, watching the constellation of red stars.

The modicum of faith that had survived in me until adulthood perished alongside my mother. I had not worshipped, prayed, or taken part in a religious celebration of any sort including Christmas mass in more than a decade. But no span of years can erase certain memories, and passages from the book of *Revelation* and many others surfaced in my mind. I recalled reading that the stars would fall, that the dead would awaken, that there would be unbelievable destruction and suffering, that panic would ensue on a scale unprecedented in all of history. In the 13th century a Jesuit monk, shaken by a vision of the final judgement, wrote: *"Blessed are the dead in Jerusalem, For the day of suffering comes as a swift wind, and their tribulations shall be to ours as but a single stone cast upon a mountainside."*

Hours into the night, I found myself walking the highway with a group of people heading to the nearby town.

At an all-night diner, I sat alone and examined my life but found no answers. If tomorrow came, what change could I make that would give meaning to my ant-like existence in a universe of ants? An unnatural hush hung over the world; something massive and unseen was absorbing the ambient sounds of everything that moved. Every conversation, every tinkle of the bell when the door opened and closed, every clink of glassware and cutlery, every wisp of paper and rattle of change on the countertop was muffled.

When dawn drew near, I started back to the campus alone and on foot, not knowing what else to do.

The sun rose, and the grounds of the college were deserted but for a handful of people in the main administrative building. When I found them in the rotunda, I stopped and tried to take stock. The windows in the high dome poured long columns of light down into the open space, highlighting the hundred-year-old crest inlaid in the marble floor. I watched motes of dust float in the yellow shafts. On the far side of this large, open space, a wall of tinted windows and doors looked out across a concrete balcony and down onto a large central courtyard where concrete walkways radiated outward from a bronze sculpture like the spokes of a wheel. Windows in all the other buildings were dark.

A man with yellow hair and a cigarette dangling from his lips stood at a display table to my left and sorted through piles of colored rags. He told me with a smirk that he was going to make bandages. As he mumbled to himself, I took note of the others who had stopped here. Some sat quietly while others paced; some wandered into and out of empty offices. A small group sat in a circle on the floor and talked quietly.

A giant flatscreen monitor was mounted on a wall above the information desk. Live reports on the deepening diplomatic crisis came over the airwaves. During the night, the Chinese Premier had called home that nation's ambassadors to the United States and the U.N., announcing at the same time that all diplomatic ties between the two countries were suspended indefinitely. Here in the U.S., every Cabinet member and most of the congressional leadership had been moved to "undisclosed locations," to underground hideouts prepared back when the threat to all life came from the Soviet Union. Every harbor was empty or near empty of merchant ships and naval vessels, the newscasts said. Nowhere in U.S. coastal waters could an American warship be found aside from floating museums like those in Mobile Bay and Pearl Harbor, or those dry-docked in Mississippi, San Diego, and Virginia. The Vice President's whereabouts were unknown to anyone outside the Executive Branch.

On the screen, the news report switched to a recorded feed from the conflict zone. The picture—transmitted from an aircraft carrier—showed a wide-angled view of the heavens. Against the washed-out backdrop of sky and distant gray clouds, a blazing object dived toward the East China Sea. It cut a blinding streak through the atmosphere and left a contrail that was miles long and pointed backward towards infinity.

A meteor? A missile?

Creeping cold enveloped me.

Had it begun? Surely, there would be some sort of official message, some warning.

One by one, the others joined me in front of the set. There were murmured questions, and then a peal of laughter erupted from one of the women. She snickered while the rest of us looked at one another and tried to discern the source of the humor that was so obvious to her. She laughed again, and her mirth grew as the report continued. Finally, she fell into a long, loud guffaw that rocked her entire body and had her wiping away tears.

Then she started screaming.

A long, bloody, terrifying scream tore out of her and unnerved the rest of us.

The panic was beginning.

Another woman, a peculiar sparkle in her brown eyes, joined the man at the table and said she would make bandages also. She looked around her as if she expected more discarded rags to appear on the floor, then she walked away saying she needed to find better fabric that she could tear into strips.

The screamer collapsed into a chair and fixed her eyes on the crest inlaid in the floor.

She did not speak again.

My own uneasiness was still in check for the moment, but I felt it moving at the back of my mind, pacing like an animal ready to bolt from a cage.

Onscreen, the reporting continued.

Russia's Ambassador to the United States had been recalled, but he and that nation's Foreign Minister continued to act as intermediaries urging the White House and Beijing to negotiate a stand-down.

Through it all, I found myself unable to accept what was happening. The visit I'd received the night before already felt distant and unreal. The news the two men brought to me was too incredible, too far outside the bounds of rationality, and my mind could not accept it, so I put it aside.

In the very real world of geopolitical conflict, there was the truth that in a matter of hours life, as we had known it might come to an end. Nearly half the world's population, the fortunate half, could be dead before nightfall. There was only one planet known to harbor intelligent life. Hours from now, it might be nothing more than a scarred and contaminated rock. That knowledge by itself touched the bounds of unreality.

But, what of violent storms that appeared and then disappeared in the blink of an eye? How had a new constellation appeared—a constellation made up of aged stars that no one had ever seen? How could a woman whom I watched die be alive again?

It could not be. Yet, somehow, it was.

The sound of sobbing broke my rumination. I turned toward the glass doors that looked out over the courtyard. A blond woman richly dressed and exuding an aura of wealth and status stood with her hands flat against the panes. Her body shook with the effort to silence her cries, but the glass bounced them back into the lobby and they drifted to where I stood. She looked like a mime, her hands pressed against tinted nothingness as if shielding her eyes from some dreadful thing on the other side.

I went to her.

"What is it?" I asked, wishing I could comfort her for no other reason than that there was so little comfort left in the world.

She pressed her forehead against the glass.

"The stars..." she said. "The stars are still out."

The sun was up now, high up above the horizon. How could stars be visible? Were they the same stars, the constellation that had appeared the night before?

Suddenly, the fear—the very same fear that I had denied and held at bay the entire night—found its way through the cracks in my defenses and wrapped itself around me with hideous strength. I wanted to run, to hide. I wanted to crawl into a sewer drain and keep crawling, down and down and down until I lost my way in cold, wet blackness. But there was no place to hide.

The woman sank to her knees, her sobs bitter and profuse.

A strange urge took hold of me then. If I could see the open sky with my own eyes, if I could see it, I might see that something held to normalcy. It was daytime; there was broad daylight outside. How could stars be visible? I had to see it in order to believe it.

I went to the door.

This was why there had been no panic. The truth was too much for anyone to absorb, not just me.

An ear-splitting squawk began pulsing from the television screen. I turned to look.

"My God," an old man moaned. "My God, my God..."

A disembodied female voice, distorted by distance and unnaturally calm, crackling with static like a 1960's analogue broadcast filled the open space.

"At 6:41a.m Eastern Standard Time, the U.S. Joint Strategic Defense Command issued an advisory to the National Security Agency indicating an attack was underway against the Chinese mainland. An alert has been issued for the following areas, and all residents are encouraged to seek shelter immediately..."

I turned away from the television and leaned against the door. Slivers of ice ran in my veins. I couldn't feel my legs, but neither could I withstand the compulsion to see with clear eyes whatever was out there.

The television continued its ominous advisory, telling everyone in the viewing area to abandon their plans to evacuate.

I pushed the door open and felt a blast of warm air on my face and hands. My legs carried me, stumbling, onto the balcony and out to the bronze railing that was as warm as a stove when I clutched it. In the distance, a flock of white birds lifted skyward like an explosion of sea spray. My eyes followed them as they rose, and I saw high above me the cool blue of the troposphere streaked and scored with violent orange and angry red clouds—a roiling field of molten lava spreading out to smother the sky. The sun was high above the trees, and the world shimmered in an eerie, undulating light. The great clock high in the bell tower across campus had stopped.

And the birds.

The gigantic flock climbed high into the air, wheeling and turning, soaring around and around above the buildings, golden light flashing through their wings. Like the inner workings of a machine, or the delicate gears of a celestial timepiece, the avian wheel spun against the horrific sky. They followed one another like automatons, like clockwork creatures precisely tuned. So perfect were the circles they described in midair, I knew they must be guided by some power beyond nature and instinct.

High in the western sky, the triad of red stars still shone with nightmarish beauty, even against the morning sky. A panicked voice called from the doorway, urging me to come back inside, but I could not go.

I had to *see*.

With my own eyes I had to see these things, even though my mind protested more loudly than it had before. Nothing I saw could be happening.

"...And I looked up, compelled to see the face of Death as it came for me, and in that moment all things were made clear..."

There would be neither war nor peace. The awful weapons of humankind—whether launched from ships, dropped from planes, or fired from underground silos—would never reach their targets., and the sun, at long last, had run its course in overseeing humanity's existence. The eye of history was closing, and the end of all things was at hand. I, like so many in every corner of the world, had simply been unable to believe.

Other people appeared in doorways and emerged from buildings I had thought deserted. I called out hoarsely to anyone who could hear me, urging them to come out and look. A wave of emotions washed through me: numbing terror, a profound and inexplicable sense of relief, a loneliness more acute than any feeling I have ever known.

I looked back at the doorway where the woman still stood and watched, then I, not wanting to die alone, held out my hand to her. She took a halting step out the door, and then another. Millions of lights appeared in the skies overhead. As she stumbled toward me, they began falling...

III.
12:26 a.m.

The beast had quieted, but it was not asleep.

I lay on my back and stared at the ceiling, a Newport Menthol smoldering between the fingers of my right hand. Outside the opened window the street was quiet, but I knew that sooner or later I'd hear a siren, or a car would roll past with its stereo blasting. The apartment, where I'd lived for two years, was on the ground floor facing the street. It was a small place, cramped some would say. The bed was next to the window, and if I sat up and looked out, I'd see the aquamarine glow of streetlights dapple through the leaves of the oak outside.

I took a drag on the Newport, held its acrid heat in my lungs, then I puffed out a single ring of smoke and watched it rise like a loop of spider thread toward the light fixture in the ceiling. The smoke ring dissolved, and as it did, I heard a car pull up to the curb outside and stop.

A great eye rolls beneath a closed lid. The beast rolls and flicks its tail.

I took a last drag on the cigarette, rolled to the edge of the bed, and sat up. The ceramic ashtray on the nightstand was as red as nail polish once upon a time. Now it was marred with burn trails and white ash. I reached over and ground out the butt, momentarily transfixed by the curl of smoke that ascended and disappeared.

The cyclic hum of the engine floated in through the window; before long it was punctuated by the sound of a door slamming and the squawk of a police radio.

I pushed my feet into worn-out gym shoes laying on the floor beside the bed.

Knock-knock-knock.

I stood up.

There was a machete between the mattress and the box spring, but I wouldn't need that for a while yet. I pulled my robe on and went down the short hallway to the living room.

Knock-knock-knock.

A cop's walkie-talkie warbled on the other side of the door.

I was calm, and I got myself into character before I slid the chain off and turned the deadbolt. In this neighborhood, people were slow to open doors at night, especially when there were cops on the other side. I twisted the knob and pulled the door all the way without hesitating. That would put the cop at ease.

"Evening officer. What's going on?"

His hair was graying at the temples. Should have been in plain clothes or sitting behind a desk, I thought. If he was patrolling down here on the graveyard shift, he was either a supervisor or a fuck-up, and the absence of stripes on his sleeve suggested the latter.

"Evening," he said and pushed the bib of his cap back from his forehead. "Sorry to bother you so late but we've got a situation out here. Would you mind clearing something up for us?"

"Glad to if I can," I said.

His partner waited beside the running car. A cone of white from the cruiser's headlamps stretched into the blue-green gloom of the street. Despite the shadows and the distance, I could tell there was someone in the back seat.

Bastard. Little prick.

"Could I bother you for some identification?" the cop asked.

"Sure. Come on in."

"I'll wait," he said.

I went back to the bedroom and got my driver's license. When I returned and handed it to him, he flipped it from front to back and studied the name.

"Misterrrr...*Day*...mer?"

"Da*hh*-mer," I said, emphasizing the *h*.

He handed it back.

"Right. Would you mind stepping out here?"

I followed him off the concrete slab of a porch and down the sidewalk to where the police cruiser sat.

"My partner and I found a young man in the park over on Eighth Street. Besides the fact he was butt naked, we couldn't understand a word he was saying. We put him in the car and tried to figure out where he lived, and this is where he brought us."

The other cop opened the door.

"Do you know this kid?"

The beast lashed its tail...

Prick. Little runt bastard.

"I know him," I said and sighed.

"So what gives?" the cop asked.

I sighed again.

"He's my...he and I..."

Pause

"What?" the cop asked. "You and he are what?"

I looked skyward, and then I locked eyes with the officer and raised one eyebrow. I said nothing.

"Oo-okay. So does he live with you?"

"Yes."

"What's his name?"

"Twi," I told them. "He's Cambodian. Can't learn English worth a shit."

A spurt of tearful babble shot out of the back seat. I fired off a retort, harsh and sharp as flint. Then I spoke to the cop again.

"We had a...you know...a spat," I told him. "Something stupid that I let get out of hand. He calls himself running away again I suppose. Only, last time he took his clothes."

The cops traded looks.

Another burst of rattling, staccato prattle assaulted us.

"He came here six months ago on a goddamn fishing boat," I said, cutting across the babble. "The Chinese offer them jobs then get them out to sea and turn them into slave laborers. When they get to this country they get sold, or sometimes just dumped off, and they wind up sleeping in doorways."

"Where'd you meet him?"

"I came out of *Sergio's* one night and saw him begging. Felt sorry for him so I bought him some food and gave him the jacket I had on." Runt bastard.

The old cop scratched his head.

"He's illegal?"

"I'm sponsoring him," I said.

The cops traded looks again, then the older one told his partner to pull the boy out.

"How old is he?"

"Nineteen," I said.

"You sure about that? He's kinda small for nineteen."

"'Twi means *runt*. It's what his family called him. Or so he says."

He was wrapped in a blanket, and he clutched it as if he were standing in ankle-deep snow. I spoke to the undersized prick in his own bird-like language, but I changed my tone to one that was soothing and tranquil: "I'll fix you," I told him. "I'll fix you real good."

He let loose a string of snotty, nasally vowels and tried to get back into the car.

"Whoa there," the partner said and kept the boy from crawling back onto the seat.

"Mr. Dhamler," the first cop said. "I guess you know people frown on this sort of stuff."

I sighed again.

"But I say consenting adults can do what they want...as long as they keep it indoors. You get my meaning?" He gave me a pointed look.

"I get it," I said.

My voice was calm, preternaturally calm, but the beast was awake, and it was coming.

"You're not gonna hear from either one of us again," I said. "I promise you that."

"Good enough," the cop said.

I spoke to the runt again, less threateningly this time. "Stop crying. I forgive you."

He sniveled and pulled back when I placed my arm around his shoulders. I spoke to him in a calm, soothing voice while the cops looked on with bored patience. Finally, he wiped his face with the blanket and drew next to me. Ungrateful little bitch. The machete under the mattress was heavier than it looked, but I had gotten good with it. Real good.

"You take care of him," the cop said as Twi walked gingerly toward the door.

"I will officer!" I called over my shoulder.

Don't you fuckin' worry. I'll take care of him.

The beast stood and bared its fangs. I smiled, and its wings enveloped me.

IV.
Not Counting Hope

1977

The old Chevy pickup trundled toward the hilltop with twelve of us chained together in the rear. It pitched us forward and back as it bumped across ruts in the ground, and we did our best to hold on, allowing our bodies to move freely with the rolling bed of the vehicle. It was a clear California day. Dry from the Santa Ana winds, but with clouds dotting the horizon. The promise of rain in the dry season brought almost as much joy as the rain itself. But that rain was still a long, long way off, if indeed it ever reached us. In contrast, a fine layer of red dust coated the truck and everything in it, people and pioneer tools (the pickaxes, sledgehammers, and shovels) that lay in the bed. We looked impassively at each other as we bounced along, no one wanting to speak.

The three women with us were dark-skinned and all had their hair tied away under blue bandanas. The bandanas did not provide as much protection from the sun as the baseball caps the men wore, but they were handy for wiping sweat out of the eyes, and for soaking with water and applying to a burning face or neck. The women wore the same tough boots that we wore though, and the same simple outfit—navy blue pants and work shirt without a belt. If they had had lighter complexions, they would have been allowed to work indoors stocking shelves or cleaning, minding children, serving food, perhaps answering telephones—even if being lighter made them no prettier. As they were, they had to labor outdoors or in factories alongside the men.

I fed my mind idle thoughts so that it would stop torturing me with the knowledge my wife had disappeared. She had been gone for two days now, and I had no idea where she was.

BILL OF SALE

Seller
Full Name: Grimes, M. T., Esq.
Street Address: Grimes Estates ZIP: 95132
City: San Jose State: California
Phone Number (#): confidential Email: contact@mtgrimes

Buyer
Full Name: Confidential
Street Address: confidential ZIP:
City: State:
Phone Number (#): Email:

Description of property: 27y female (D. Theresa Laviscoli-Grimes)

- Accountant / Office Assistant
- 0 children, illnesses, impairments

Purchase price: $ 158,687.00

I, the undersigned **Seller**, agree to sell the above described personal property for the purchase price and certify that all of the information contained in this document is true and accurate to the best of my knowledge.

I the undersigned **Buyer**, recognize this document as a receipt for the personal property in exchange for the purchase price. I understand that the personal property is being sold in "as is" condition and that after the sale I will agree not to hold the Seller liable for any found defects.

ACKNOWLEDGMENT OF NOTARY PUBLIC

There was an empty ache in the hollow of my chest, a slow panic that I had at first kept controlled but that was now becoming unbearable. She had not run off, because she would not have run without me, of that I was certain. I had waited all weekend for her to show up, listened for the click of her heels in the front room. When the first bell sounded this morning, she still had not come home.

She is very light. Perhaps not light enough to pass when the sun browns her in summer, but very close, and she has thick brown hair that hangs past her shoulders. She is also educated. Not merely literate, as we all are more or less, but educated. She speaks three languages fluently and is conversant in a fourth. Her handwriting is a beautiful blend of calligraphy and Arabesque curls and loops. She plays the piano. She can do Algebraic equations, calculate interest and percentages, do long division and calculate the volume and surface area of three-dimensional shapes in her head. She has tried to teach me algebra and basic geometry on quiet winter evenings, but none of it stays with me. Darling would bring a handsome profit to a kidnapper. But God forbid she should fall into the hands of some ignoramus who would put her to work on an assembly line or sit her behind a cash register. God forbid it, for doing such work would kill her as surely as falling off a cliff would. She cannot tolerate tedium and repetition.

Even worse would be to place her in a private residence, for she would doubtlessly face the greatest danger of all, the one far, far worse than boredom.

Though she loved dresses and dressing up, Darling (that is her real name, Darling Teresa Lavascoli, given to her at birth and only lately changed to Grimes) would often wear pants to hide herself and preserve her modesty. She has exquisite legs, and for most of the years we've known each other, we've managed to keep this our secret. If she is put to work in someone's household her secret will very quickly become known, and those legs will help bring about her undoing. She always says she will kill herself first, so that she will not have to suffer through it. And if she cannot kill herself beforehand, she'll kill him (whoever he might be) afterward. She told me long ago that I must always be prepared to go on without her, that that's how life is for those like us.

The acute ache in my chest twisted like a knife, and a raw, anguished cry reverberated inside my head.

Not my Darling. Please dear God, not her. And I remembered all the other wives I knew or had heard of who had suffered that same awful fate.

Was my own mother one? I never knew anything about her, and it bothered me more and more as I grew up. Every year on my birthday, I found myself staring into the mirror and wondering how much of what I saw was her.

I know my father well. Not my real father, I guess I should say, but the man to whom I was given to raise. He was the handyman, mechanic, gardener, and chauffeur on the place where I grew up, and he told me that he had been given a second wife shortly after I came along and my mother was sold. Was he my mother's husband then, I had wondered? He had never answered when I asked him that, telling me only to mind the present and not go worrying about the past.

When my wife did not come home two nights ago, I imagined she had been kept at the office complex not far from home where she worked in the accounting division of Grime's corporation. Mainly because her skin is light, the police would have been lenient with her if she had been out after curfew with only her ID and no pass. She would have told them that she had worked late, and they would have allowed her to go on her way without question.

Besides her complexion, Darling had other tricks that helped her get her way. She had poise and could affect an imperious air that made people, White and Black, pause before addressing her. Three months ago, we had spent a Sunday afternoon at the markets. When we were ready to head home, Darling, instead of getting into the long line for the bus, walked to a taxi stand and put her hand out. I stood next to her, trying not to let my nervousness show, wanting to go to the bus line because it had been a good day and all I wanted now was to get home without incident. She told me not to worry and waved at an approaching taxi. A policeman came along just as the cab pulled to the curb. He asked Darling for her ID card and glared at her when she held it up between thumb and forefinger but would not give it to him. Reassured that she too was Black, he asked us if we thought we were too good to ride the bus. He reached for her elbow, ready to turn us away from the cabstand. Darling drew her arm away and, peering at him above her glasses, told him not to touch her. I watched the ire flood into his face, and I knew we would both be arrested and fined. We hadn't done anything. There were no Whites waiting, so it wasn't illegal for us to stand there and hail a cab. But he would have made up a reason for placing us under arrest by the time a radio car arrived, and they would have made up even more by the time they got us to the station. Darling straightened her back, pushed the glasses up on her nose and gave the man as condescending a look as had ever passed between two human beings. She told him who her "employer" was (she would not use the word *holder*, and *owner* was completely out of the question) and then quoted the city ordinance that covered public and commercial transport. She said there was no reason she could not hail a taxi, and if an incident as minor as this one were dragged out and somehow caused her to be late for work tomorrow, her "employer" would make certain that cop and everyone in his chain of command appeared before the Mayor's council to explain the police policy of harassing innocent workers who only wanted to get home before curfew. The policeman had stared at her with pure hatred then walked off muttering to himself.

Usually, if an enslaved who worked the day shift was caught out after seven o'clock without a pass to a specific destination, he or she went straight to the tombs—the catacombs of holding cells below the city—until the holder came to post bail. Most "employers," or holders ("owners" actually, but that term had fallen into disfavor during the Human Rights Movement of the late 60's) passed the cost of bail and the resulting fine on to the enslaved person. And there were other punishments: additional withholdings, demotions, extra work. Any number of tactics including beatings (which, though not talked about in polite company and denied in the media, still occurred). It would not have taken her more than an hour to walk from her building, but I—idiot that I am—did not go out to look for her until it was almost ten.

The truck hit a dip in the road and lurched to a stop. Red dust swirled around us. The doors opened and two men climbed out of the cab. One was young and stocky and wore a black goatee to add years to his cherub face. The other, the older of the two men, had a red mustache and wore a camouflage boonie hat with a wide, floppy brim and a leather drawstring that hung down from his chin. He was our overseer.

It seemed to me that he did not like this job. I guessed he did it because he lacked either the skills or the connections to gain a position that would give him the same authority in a different arena. He walked out a few feet and surveyed the landscape, then told the other one to lower the tailgate. He turned to us and said, "Okay folks, on your feet."

We climbed down from the truck one-by-one, moving awkwardly around the digging tools. When we were all on the ground, the younger man freed us from the wrist manacles but left us chained together at the ankles.

"I'm sorry about the shackles gang, but Mr. Grimes is in a strange mood this week. And we all know, what the boss wants, he gets." He paused as if he expected us to show we appreciated his commiseration. His assistant nodded. "Anyway," he went on, "what I need from y'all is a slit trench. About four foot deep...from that orange marker way up there," he pointed. "All the way down to that trunk pipe."

We followed his gaze down the side of the hill to a spot nearly one hundred meters away. He was going to use twelve people for an entire day to dig a trench that a backhoe could make in a couple of hours. *How stupid is this?* I thought but kept the thought to myself. The slope was probably too steep for a backhoe, or Grimes was too cheap to hire one, which made no sense because the contractor who supplied the pipe would undoubtedly be equipped to dig the trench where it would lay.

The overseer looked at me, and I wondered if my face had given away my thoughts.

"It's gonna be rough going in spots because of boulders. When we come across one, we're gonna have to team up and break it out. Until we find the first one, I want four of you to start with picks and the other eight with shovels. We'll trade off after a while."

Grimes was an idiot. We all knew it, and we all knew that they knew how we felt and felt the same way. Why in God's name did the man want to irrigate a hillside filled with boulders? The overseer started toward the truck then stopped and said, "Probably would go quicker if we'd brought in a backhoe, but it's good we got plenty of work to keep everybody busy." He was saying the more work we did, the less chance someone would be sold at the end of the quarter.

We trudged up the hillside and set to work.

I took up a pickaxe and for four hours both the noises in my head and the pain in my chest subsided. Hard physical labor is a wonderful stress reliever...depending on how much stress there was to begin with and whether or not the tools of ones work readily change into weapons. My muscles worked like carefully oiled machine parts though a fire smoldered in my gut. I lost myself in the task, but slowly, insidiously, the diminished ache inside me crept up again. Four and a half hours and forty-one meters down the hillside the chattering in my mind resumed, despite my labor. Our rhythm was broken by a sizable chunk of rock buried in the dirt. When we had removed it, I took up the pickaxe again. On my second swing, Bailey, the man chained to my left leg, threw himself to the ground and away from me.

"Heeey, man! Watch how you swing that damned thing!"

Everyone stopped and looked at me.

"Sorry," I said and offered my hand to help him up. We went back to work, and I tried to chop into the dirt more carefully. After a few more strokes, however, I caught myself grunting like a madman on each swing, and I realized I was slinging the pickaxe as though I intended to cleave the planet into two. The howling, the screaming in my mind grew until it drowned out all other thoughts. The anxiety lodged in my chest spread like poison from a ruptured organ. I was hurling the pick with such violence that it wedged itself into the ground on every other stroke. The others gave me as wide a berth as the chains allowed. The sun was directly overhead when I heard my name being shouted from far away.

"Benjamin! *Benjamin!*"

I looked up, dazed.

"You trying to kill somebody?" the overseer asked. He and his assistant stood nearby—out of range of the pick.

"I've got work to do," I said breathlessly. "Leave me alone."

"You're gonna give yourself a heart attack if you don't take it easy," the overseer replied. "Why don't you take a break? It's almost time for lunch anyway."

The others were watching me.

"Leave me alone," I said again. "I've got work to do."

I swung the pick and buried its head in the dirt again.

"Dadgummit! You're gonna break that thing if you don't quit swinging it that way!"

"Hell with it," I said. "He'll just buy another."

"Okay. Lunch!" the overseer called.

The others looked warily at me.

The weather had been mild that morning, but now the sun blazed like a planet-smelting furnace. I had worked the entire time without noticing how fiercely hot the air was becoming. Now it hit me all at once, and I leaned on the ax handle trying to collect my thoughts and grit my way through a sudden bout of dizziness. A band of intense pressure settled around my forehead and temples. My ears buzzed, and my lips tingled. I shook my head but could not clear it. One minute I was angry but fine physically; the next moment, darkness seeped around the edges of my sight and worked its way inward until I saw only a blurred circle of brightness. I heard Darling laugh, and for the first time I wanted to cry out loud.

The ground swayed and I lowered myself to one knee. I was sinking into a well of blackness, but my whole mind was focused on my wife. Hands grabbed me trying to hold me up even as I tried to lie down. Where was she? Where was she? Some sonofabitch on this place knew what had happened to her. Wasn't I worth a sideways whisper letting me in on the secret? If she was kidnapped, didn't that fucking bastard Grimes care enough to notify the authorities at least? Wasn't she worth that much?

"Help him. Take his arms."

"Move him out of this sun."

She could do computations in her head that most people needed a calculator for. Were they going to let some dirty fucking rafficker steal her and drag her off somewhere to count boxes, or sort eggs, or clean fish?

I found myself lying in the dirt, water draining from my nose and eyes. Where was she?

"Heat exhaustion," someone said. "He's l' delirious with it."

They called my name and faces pressed close to mine.

"Get on the radio and call for doc. No, wait...unlock him first."

From far off, I felt the manacles let go of my leg. A cold, wet cloth touched my forehead. I grabbed the hand that held the bandanna and felt another one stroke my hair. More hands took my other hand and rubbed it, trying to comfort me.

"Let it out..." the first woman said. "Let it out."

She knew something. Was she the only one who had missed seeing Darling the past two days? Most of the women hated her because she worked indoors and wore heels. She got a new suit every month. She went to meetings with Grimes and sat in when his business partners came to the estate. She and I were the first to have a television. Where other estates worked, we got Veteran's Day and Memorial Day off because of her, yet the others hated her. They must have known something. They *had* to know she was gone. They had to. But they said nothing because they were glad. Anger flared alongside my sorrow; still, I clung to the woman's hand as if it were Darling's own.

"Doc's on his way up," the younger man said.

The overseer knelt beside me. "It's gonna be all right," I heard him say. "Margaret, Tess, go on and get something to eat. He'll be all right."

They put me in the back of doc's station wagon, and he drove me down the hill and back to where the residences were, stopping at the large shed that served as a dispensary. "Doc" was actually a registered nurse, which was cheaper than having a real doctor but smarter than having no qualified medical personnel at all on an estate this size. He checked my blood pressure and my pulse, listened to my heart, then drove an IV needle into my arm and connected it to a bag of saline.

"So what happened up there?" he asked.

Doc's tone was just right for a medical person; he cared but he didn't care. He'd move heaven and hell to see you through your illness, but if you happened to die anyway, he'd go home, eat his dinner, drink a beer, and fall asleep in front of the television.

"You wanna talk?" he asked when I said nothing. A picture of Grimes hung on the wall above his desk, the same picture that hung in all our living rooms. I stared at it in uncustomary and undisguised hatred.

I cleared my throat.

"Someone...someone took Darling."

"Who's Darling?"

He was still new here, had been on the place less than a month but still he should have known who she was. His tone surprised me, however. For an instant, he sounded genuinely concerned. But I reminded myself that it was part of his job.

"My wife," I said. "Someone took my wife."

"How do you know?"

I focused on the ceiling tiles and tapped my foot against the air, straining to keep my grief out of my voice.

"Why else would she not come home for two nights?"

"Did you call her job?"

I tapped harder. Perhaps he meant no harm. But how stupid was that question? If his wife had been missing for two days, would he not have called her job?

"I called," I said finally. "She's gone."

Doc said he would see what he could find out and sent me home on one day's bed rest later that afternoon. That night, the clock in the hall chimed twelve, and I was wide awake on the bed, clutching Darling's bathrobe and gazing at a corner of the ceiling when a knock rattled the panes in the front door. I went to the door and saw the overseer standing like a jaundiced statue in the urine-colored light from a bulb that promised not to draw insects.

"Benjamin? How you feeling?"

"All right I guess," I said flatly.

He cleared his throat.

"I came to give you some news. She ain't kidnapped. She ain't hurt or nothing either."

My heart jumped in my chest. His words were like cold water on a fresh burn. She was okay. I nearly smiled but caught myself. Where was she? What else was there?

I waited for him to continue.

"Mr. Grimes took her with him when he went down to San Diego on Friday." He paused, guessing I already knew what would come next.

I waited.

"Well..." he scratched his chin. "He left her down there Benjamin. Traded her..."

A great iron bell clanged inside my head.

He traded her. He traded her.

Traded...

He *sold* her. The black-hearted sonofabitch *sold* my wife. No matter how they dressed it up...traded, transferred, optioned, re-assigned…it was all the same. They bought and sold people the way they did pets and furniture, as if a person were nothing more than a used car or an old painting in a frame. As if Darling were a piece of office equipment. And the man standing before me could not bring himself to say the word, could not keep himself from sugarcoating her fate.

"You can call her," he added and handed me a piece of paper. "I'll have one of the others check in on you tomorrow. Be ready for work on Wednesday. Oh-five-hundred." He turned and stepped off the porch without a backward glance.

I closed the door and went into the kitchen where I snatched the phone from its cradle and dialed the number. It rang and rang and rang until I wondered if he had written it down wrong. I was about to hang up when a tired voice answered.

"Women's dorm."

I spoke rapidly, not sure if the woman on the other end understood me.

"Hold on," she said when I paused. The phone clunked onto a hard surface, and I waited through a long, unnerving silence. I was *this* close to hearing her. What was happening on the other end?

"Benjamin!" Her voice jumped out at me; her breath whistled into the line. "Benjamin, Benjamin…." She was crying. "Benjamin…you have to come…you have to get me out of here."

"Where are you? Did they hurt you?'

She hiccupped.

"Talk to me," I said. "What happened?"

"You have to get me away from here. You have to talk to Mr. Grimes."

"Darling, tell me what happened. Where are you?"

"S-San Diego," she said. "I'm at a mill in San Diego."

Evidently, Grimes had taken her with him when he went to meet the president of a company that manufactured sports attire. The man had been so impressed with Darling that he offered Grimes a queen's ransom for her once the meeting was over. Grimes, needless to say, was not at all sentimental when it came to business. Moreover, he was a greedy piece of filth who would have sold his own mother had she been Black. Grimes had "traded" Darling to this man, who wanted to make her his *personal assistant*—a euphemism for a concubine who actually works during the day. Darling was outraged. She told the man she was a human being and a married woman. He might as well shoot her right then and there if he thought she would ever let him touch her. And then she had told Grimes—pointedly—that she was ready to come home.

A person who could afford Darling wouldn't be stupid enough to do her real harm, no matter how she behaved, but the man Grimes left her with had other ideas. He'd had her taken to a manufacturing plant where truckloads of noxious chemicals were cooked and spun into synthetic fiber for giant bolts of cloth that were shipped to clothing plants in Asia. When she got there, her suit was taken away, and she had been given a pair of overalls and a bandanna with which to tie her hair. Then they took her to the floor of the plant where gigantic, five-hundred-gallon vats were used to cook the different chemical compounds. She and the unfortunate women in that crew would climb inside the vats and clean them by hand. The chemical residue was caustic and highly toxic. Even with a respirator, she said, she had not been able to breathe after only a few minutes. The chemical oversuit the women wore was heavy and stifling. Late in the day, she had watched them drag the body of one woman out. They made her work the entire day without a break and made her sleep on the break room floor at the end of the twelve-hour shift. She had been given a cold sandwich from a vending machine for dinner and was told she could get water from a tap in one of the broom closets off the factory floor. Her supervisor—a blond-haired, broad-shouldered Nazi frau of a woman—had slapped her when she dared to ask if she could call home.

The people who raised Darling and those who worked her had always had one thing in common: they protected her. She had always been favored, always been given first choice; she had never been struck as far as I knew.

Now she wept bitterly. "She *hit* me! All I did was ask..."

They had not allowed her to call home, nor given her two minutes to scribble a note to me so that I would know she was alive. Friday evening and Friday night, all day Saturday, all day Sunday, all day Monday, they had worked her mercilessly. This was her first night in the worker's dormitory. It was just after midnight, and she would have to get back up at four a.m. for the morning shift. The abject misery in her voice made my own eyes burn with rage.

"They're going to kill me... They want to break my spirit, but they're going to kill me first..."

She couldn't help being who she was. Darling was willful; she was entitled. She was unaccustomed to ill treatment. If she were kept there, it was possible she would survive. And if she survived, she might one day be put to work doing something that utilized her gifts. But that didn't make it better. There was no way. There was no way on God's earth I would leave her to suffer in that place. I would kill Grimes. I would kill every cop, every guard, every rich degenerate on the face of the earth if I had to.

I would die if I had to.

"I'm coming," I said, not knowing where she was, or where we would go from there, but knowing I had no choice. I had tomorrow for bed rest, so I'd have one day, or nearly a full day's head start. I wouldn't be able to get on an airplane. And how many checkpoints could I get through if I stole a car and tried to drive? A bus was the only thing that would even get me close to her. After I found her, where could I take her so that we would be safe? Mexico, obviously. But how many people died in the southwestern deserts each year trying to slip across the border into Mexico? It would be much easier to cross the northern border into Canada. But Canada was so far away. There were old tales about a network of sympathizers who had helped people escape to freedom in the 1800s when parts of the U.S. still outlawed slavery. Abraham Lincoln, the sixteenth President, had prepared an Executive Order freeing all slaves but had torn it up when every state in the south and six in the Midwest threatened to declare themselves an independent nation. If those networks had ever been real, they had long ago disbanded or been shut down. There would be no one to help us. Once we cleared the fence, so to speak, we would be on our own and would either find freedom or die. Captured fugitives had the shortest life expectancy of any people on earth. Most died mysteriously in police custody, or shortly after they were returned to their holders. Better to get rid of them once they started running.

"I'm coming," I said again. "You hold on. I'll come get you."

"Get off that phone!" A fierce voice cracked like a whip in the air behind her. "Hang it up. *Now!*"

"*Benjamin help me! Hurry!*"

I heard struggling, someone trying to rip the phone out of her hands.

"Benjamin!"

The line went dead, and I clutched the receiver until my hand shook. A blister of pain, like a dollop of red-hot metal, formed in my throat and stuck there. I slammed the receiver down on the countertop, pounding and pounding it until it broke apart in my hand. Blinded by fury, I ripped the base off the wall and hurled it across the room. There were four chairs at the small kitchen table. I grabbed one and, hefting it like a two-handled club, I went into the living room and laid into the portrait of Grimes. Soon, splintered wood and bits of glass littered the floor. A gaping hole yawned in the wall. I went around the room and destroyed everything: the shelves, the bookcase, the other pieces of furniture, the television, everything. The chair itself splintered finally when I struck a beam in the sheetrock.

I sank to the floor with dark spots dancing in front of my eyes, my hands shaking, my heart slamming against my chest. A minute passed. Two minutes. Then I rose and made my way to the bedroom where I found my pants and pulled them on. What hope did we have? I first had to get myself to San Diego; then I had to find her. I would find the place, but how would I get her out? I didn't know how we would make it to Canada, or even to Mexico without a miracle. It was useless to hope.

Useless. And, not counting hope, not counting on a distant and uncaring God to help us, what else did we have? Nothing.

I grabbed my shirt and my boots. I gathered all the money we had in the house and shoved it into my pockets. All I knew was that I had to find her; I had to get her away from that place, or I had to die trying.

V.

Apparitions

Boston, Massachusetts
October 1888

"It's that house," the woman whispered. "And those Blessington's. That house did something to them, or they did something to it."

The skin of her face was lined and limp; the dark stain of burst capillaries circled both her eyes. She wasn't an old woman, but she looked as if she had seen a lifetime's worth of horrors in the span of only a few months. She touched the pewter crucifix that dangled from a chain around her neck.

"The first ones, the ones who came over from England, had second sight; they could feel stuff and see it plain as day—before it happened. And old Mister Blessington, the boy's father, well, he was evil to begin with. He said he believed in freedom for the Coloreds, but still he looked on 'em like they were trainable pets instead of human folk. He would buy them out of bondage in the South but, once he got them here, he would put 'em to work in his mill, or in that house, and they couldn't leave. *Pets* they were to him, pets with a set of hands that he could put to work while he told himself he was doing something righteous. And he kept right on doing that, even after his son left. Even after the Abolitionists got wind and tried to make him stop. Yes sir, he kept right on lying to himself and to the good Lord. Right up until those twins came."

She paused.

"It was...wrong. That birth I mean. Everything about it was wrong."

She swallowed.

"The last Colored he lured to that house was a washerwoman who was in a family way. She was close to her time when she came there, but...God as my witness, she was already past her birthing years, *way past*. She was withered and wrinkled, her face and hands; her hair was grayer than mine is, and on the night she gave birth...my God. She was dark, but those twins came out gray and sickly looking. Not half-White mind you, but gray like wood ash, with something brown and gummy clinging all over...and no cord. It was awful." She buried her face in her hands. "It was so awful. I was in the room, and I didn't know whether to cry or scream when I saw 'em. When Mr. Blessington...my God...when he came in and saw how terrible it was, he tied them up in an old quilt and carried them down to the root cellar. I reckon he thought they'd die before the night was over because he left it there. Then he had the manservant drag the pallet out to the backyard and set fire to it."

Her voice quivered.

"She was gone the next morning. I don't know what happened to her or where she went, but she was gone like she had never been there. Those two didn't die, neither. They didn't. They survived somehow. Down there in that dark, they started *growing*. The next morning, he opened the doors and went down there, and then he came rushing back up all out of breath. And then he wanted *me* to go down there and look. *Me!* But I wouldn't go, by the Lord Jesus. 'Don't be alarmed' he said to me. Don't be alarmed? *Do* be alarmed. My God...be terrified..."

She gripped the crucifix.

"I told him I wouldn't. God as my witness, I told him I'd leave that house without a backward glance if he tried to make me. And I should have left there anyway, like his son did. I should have left.

"There were times in the middle of the night, when I heard knocking on the cellar doors. Knocking, on and off, all through the night. The windows were open on the back of the house, and I could hear it plain.

"Well, he got the shotgun next day and went back down. I stood on the porch and watched while him and the manservant pulled those doors open and went down the steps. Then I heard that gun go off, twice. He came back up to get a shovel."

Her bloodless face became whiter as she spoke. The blue weave of veins in her neck pulsed against her pallor.

"But after he buried them...*they would still get up!* At night, I would hear them knocking on those doors. His wife spent the last year of her life scared to death. When her husband took sick, she knew it was something that would end him, and she went to the priest and got a bottle of holy water. The next day, she dressed herself for a funeral, but she went out back and sprinkled that water all around. She got on her knees in front of those doors, and she stayed there 'til she fainted from heat. I had to drag her back inside the house myself.

"When she came too, she got the manservant to chain those doors shut and put a great big padlock on them. From that day to her last on this earth, she didn't go nowhere inside that house without a Bible in her hand..."

Boston, 3 months earlier

Her first night in the old house passed without incident.

Cecilia Blessington had come to the spacious home near Beacon Hill for the first time in her life with the solemn purpose of settling her grandparents' estate. The pair had died under strange circumstances, almost simultaneously, it was believed, and she was their named beneficiary.

The conditions surrounding her inheritance were unusual: she was twenty-four, unmarried, and still living under her father's roof in Hammersmith in the north of Greater London. It was rare for a woman to be beneficiary to such a windfall, and rarer still for her to undertake a long trip for business where she, and not her husband or father, was the principal stakeholder. To travel alone across the ocean for such business was unheard of, but the independent, headstrong, and fearless Cecilia had made the trip on her own nonetheless and, in doing so, she became her father's financial equal.

She stuffed the crinkly mop of her auburn hair into the ruffles of a slumber cap. After saying her prayers, she climbed onto the plush, four-poster bed that was large enough to sleep an entire family. Her grandparents' bed. Her last thought as she drifted toward sleep was of her ten-year-old sister, Catherine, on whom she doted, and toward whom she felt as strong a maternal instinct as she would have had she given birth to the child instead of their mother. She would bring Catherine to see this city one day, or she would send her to the Sorbonne in Paris to study art. Whatever the younger girl wished, Cecilia would see that it was done.

Both girls were duplicates of their mother Camille, an extraordinarily beautiful woman who had been born a slave in Jamaica.

The man who would become Cecilia's grandfather, a Boston textile merchant who had visited the island often in the long-ago years before the war, had first seen the uncommonly beautiful child in the home of an associate during one of his many stays. After much haggling and persuading, he arranged to buy the girl, who was then twelve, and he took her back to Massachusetts where he freed her, ostensibly.

Though she could have walked away from the household any time she wished, the girl was alone in a strange land, still a child in all respects, and so dependent upon the merchant for the bare necessities of life that she, in fact, remained little more than a slave. Because her "benefactor" was nearly devoid of certain drives, she was safe in one important regard. But he made up for his impotence with ruthlessness, and it took no effort at all to coerce the girl into working for a penny a week as a chambermaid. When two Abolitionists came to his door with a policeman one day, determined to take the girl away from him, Blessington had called her into the parlor and left her alone to speak with them. In answering their questions, the girl disclosed that she had her own bed and was never harassed; she received two meals a day, and she was given a wage—pittance though it was. The policeman had informed the rescuers that their charge against Blessington was baseless. The girl remained in the house and, later—after she showed adroitness with a needle and thread—she began repairing her mistress's clothing.

It was the merchant's son and only child, Bernhard Blessington, likewise twelve when Camille came to the household, who had befriended her and who, over the decade that followed, fell madly in love with the shy, beautiful girl.

For years, they managed with care and deception to keep their burgeoning affection hidden from his sometimes benign, sometimes spiteful parents.

A week after Bernhard's twenty-second birthday, he announced that after working in his father's business for four years, he wanted to leave home and go to Cambridge, where he would take up the study of business at Harvard. It was on the night of his announcement that he went up to the attic to visit Camille and found her curled on her narrow cot weeping into her pillow. Assuming he knew the source of her distress, he assured her he would come back often and would think only of her in the time between visits. But she told him it was not the loss of his love that she feared; she was crying because she was with child, and once he was gone from the house, she had no idea what would happen to her.

Another week passed, and Bernhard broke the news to his parents over dinner, telling them he would forego Harvard and marry Camille despite her race and regardless of what the law said. On that night, raised voices and the sounds of crashing and breaking were heard throughout the house. The next morning, with dawn scarcely in the eastern sky, Bernhard crept to the attic again and awakened Camille. They bundled her belongings into a satchel, and then they left the house together, never to return.

They arrived in London a month later, in the spring of 1864, and Bernhard found a clergyman who, swayed by her tears and by his earnest pleas, capitulated and married the pair. Bernhard renounced his American citizenship and pledged allegiance to the Crown, thus returning the family name to England more than two hundred years after it had departed.

With what remained of the cache of gold coins he had stolen from his father's drawing room, he purchased a snug cottage in the East End and turned its main room into a modest fabric boutique. The tiny "shop" quickly established a clientele of neighborhood women. In time, it earned enough money to pay for a real storefront near the market at Spitalfields.

The child Camille carried was born in perfect health, and she thrived in the safe, loving environment her parents had painstakingly fashioned for her. By her tenth year, Cecilia had insinuated herself into her father's daily routine, leaving for the shop with him each morning. She would play and amuse herself but, to the delight of customers, she would also set her dolls aside so that she could sweep the shop or dust while her father attended to them. Her mother, who was often commissioned to create garments from the purchased fabrics, would appear at lunchtime every day, and the family would have a quiet meal in the back room. After the mid-day repast, her father would re-open the shop and return to his duties while her mother gave Cecilia lessons in spelling, arithmetic, and geography.

Largely, wherever they went, the family was greeted with indifference, and that was a blessing in the eyes of her parents. There were times, however, when the actions of other people puzzled Cecilia tremendously.

As she watched from the front window of the shop one day, a tall man who resembled her father except for his broad shoulders shoved a Black woman into the street, where she stumbled and fell against a moving carriage. Her offense had been stopping in front of him at the corner and gazing at a colorful arrangement of tropical fruits set up beneath a bright red awning. The woman had escaped serious injury, but Cecilia had felt a bewildering rush of shame. She had fought back tears even though she had no idea who the woman was, and though she herself was safe in her father's store.

From her place in the confused world of the racially ambiguous, she had tried as much as a child might to understand something her mother had told her. They shared some of the same blood as the woman Cecilia had seen that day, she and the other much darker men and women who took pains to avoid attention as they worked and went about their daily lives. As a teen, she had begun to understand that the relative civility shown to her family was due more to her mother's extravagant beauty than to fairness and moral decency.

For all her beauty and the power it might have given her over others, Camille Blessington remained a timorous and fearful woman throughout her life. She was still a slave in her mind Cecilia often thought, as she herself became a woman. She grew angry when she remembered the afternoons her mother had spent hidden in the back of the shop, out of sight of the customers when Cecilia's lessons were done; how, on the walk home, she would take her daughter's hand and walk behind her husband much as a nurse would.

Cecilia had taken all of her physical attributes from her mother: the ravishing face and bright eyes, the supple figure, but she had also been blessed with her father's intrepid nature. Her willfulness and wiles in combination were too strong even for him to resist, and when the matter of the inheritance came up, she was able to twist his arm until he agreed that she would travel to claim it.

On her second night in the house, she heard pounding from somewhere outside, and then a floor downstairs began to creak.

She was inclined to dismiss both noises at first: perhaps a deranged neighbor was building something in the dead of night, and her own house was very likely settling. However, she soon became aware of a disturbing regularity in the creaking: it would start; then it would stop; then it would start again. It stopped altogether after a time, but then she heard a heavy object slide across the floor and bump against the wall at the foot of the stairs. Moments later, she heard—and felt—something moving in the hallway outside her bedroom door. Had she been a jumpy woman (like her mother), these stirrings would have driven her mad. As it was, they were a bit unnerving, even for her.

She took a deep breath to calm her nerves, then she got out of bed and lit the candle on the nightstand. The room was spacious. Shadows moved in the far corners when she walked to the door.

The knob rattled loosely when she took hold of it. She gave it a turn.

The door pulled open soundlessly. There was no one outside, and there was nothing to be seen when she peered around the doorframe.

Holding the candle in front of her, she stepped into the hallway.

The other doors on the second level were closed tight, so she tiptoed to the head of the stairs and looked down. More shadows leaned and pointed at odd angles, dancing in the glow of the candle, but she saw nothing out of place.

She held the candle out over the open space beyond the banister. Cold air brushed her neck and she turned suddenly, toppling the candle from its holder. She grabbed it before it fell, steadied it, and then she went to the first door on the level and pushed it to see if it would open. It did not, and so she went to each of the others and did the same thing, checking to see which was unsecured.

They were all closed tightly, and when she set her toes against the crack at the bottom of each, she felt no air circulating. She went back to her bedroom and pushed its door tight, making sure the latch clicked. Then she blew out the candle and went back to bed.

On the third night, there were more sounds.

She was shaken this time, and she lay still and listened until the noises subsided and she was able to fall back to sleep.

When she heard feet on the stairs the fourth night, she was truly terrified. She pushed herself into the corner where the bed met the wall and watched the dark room until the sun came up.

On the previous mornings, after the noises began, Cecilia had arisen and walked out of her bedroom expecting to find chaos and signs of destruction throughout the house. The odd banging and thumping, the crashes and scrapings should have left every floor and wall on the first level marred and damaged. In the daylight, she found no indication that anyone—or anything—had been in the house the night before. She wondered if her imagination were not coming to life in the darkness and running wild to the point of near madness. Unlikely, since the noises continued even after she was fully awake and even after she had arisen to investigate them. Moreover, she knew in her heart that the sounds were genuine, which bothered her in a way few things had ever been able to before. Whatever their source, the noises were real.

She opened the bedroom curtains the following night, pulling them back as far as they would go so that light from the flickering gas lamps in the street might make the room less ominous when the creaking began. She was deep in a dream about home when the curious, heavy slap of bare feet on the stairs roused her. The thin glow from outside made the room brighter than it had been on the previous nights, but the effect of this, she quickly realized, was exactly the opposite of what she had wanted. The knowledge that she would now *see* the source of the noises frightened her in a way she had not anticipated. The ludicrous idea of getting up and quickly closing the curtains occurred to her; instead, she crawled to the corner again and clutched the quilt to her drawn up knees, peeking out from behind it like a small child. The footsteps paused at the top of the stairs then turned toward her door.

The knob rattled.

A dark crack appeared and grew to a gaping maw as the door swung soundlessly on its hinges. She realized she had stopped breathing just before she blacked out, and the last thing she knew for certain was that the doorway was not empty, even though she could not name the thing that stood there.

She awoke the next morning with an agonizing pain in her neck. Her body had been wedged into the corner and held upright the entire night while her head had lolled. Wincing in pain, she dressed and went down to the kitchen where she found an open window overlooking the yard and, beyond it, the narrow alley that dustmen and refuse gatherers used in their daily to-and-fro.

This could certainly explain the feet on the stairs.

In fact, it could explain almost everything that had happened since she had come into the house.

She had business to attend to, but she decided she would go to the authorities first and report the odd doings. Now that she had a reasonable explanation for the noises, she could talk to someone official without seeming daft, and then, perhaps, she could look forward to a good night's sleep. Scavengers and pilferers had probably entered the house shortly after her grandparents' death six months earlier. Why they had never taken anything was a mystery, but clearly, their objective now was to frighten her and perhaps drive her away. If they were not coming in to steal though, why bother to invade this old house each night? Did someone think frightening her was good sport? Was it someone who still held a grudge against her grandparents? If so, it was quite a bit late to take revenge on them.

Her grandparents' passing had been peaceful in a macabre way. The housekeeper, a diminutive woman who had worked for many years in the Blessington household, had found them side-by-side on the bed and gone for the undertakers. When the funeral director and his assistant had arrived to remove the bodies, they had both been overcome by the sense that something was not as it should be. Neither had ever seen a more unusual circumstance in all their years of preparing the lifeless for the grave.

The couple's hands had been joined as if they had simply fallen asleep. There had been no visible signs of injury, no evidence of poisoning or foul play that either man could detect, but something had not been right in what they were able to see. They had decided to summon the police and the medical examiner before moving the bodies, and so they had spent the better part of that morning in the kitchen with the maid, sipping tea, and waiting.

The coroner thought they had simply lain down together and decided to die. The old man had taken ill some time before, and his passing would not have been a surprise, but the coroner surmised that if he had indeed died first, then the woman must have climbed into bed beside him and willed herself to die as well. Deaths in close proximity were not unheard of among elderly couples, but he had never seen death *summoned* in such a deliberate manner without the use of some poison or destructive agent. Moreover, like the undertaker, the medical examiner had found no hint of a substance that the woman might have taken to hasten her death. She had simply closed her eyes, it seemed, and expired.

There was no family besides the son who now lived in Britain and some distant cousins whom the maid thought still lived in the Deep South. It had therefore fallen to the couple's attorney and executor, a Mr. J.M. Philbert, Esq., to make funeral arrangements and notify the absent son of his parents' final wishes.

Bernhard and Camille Blessington had been horrified at the thought of Cecilia sailing to America alone, but their daughter had insisted she was able to fend for herself. On the day the telegram arrived telling Cecilia of her inheritance, the family had been gathered in the parlor over tea. While her little sister played the piano, the three adults had discussed the message's implications. His parents, as expected, had left nothing to Bernhard, but they had not only acknowledged his daughter, they had made her their sole heir.

The discussion was peaceful until the subject of travel arose. Cecilia had intimated that she might make the journey alone, and when she did, Bernhard had put his foot down and forbidden it. Cecilia had looked her father square in the eye and put her own foot down in turn. She had told him that she would go without his permission if need be, and as she was older than twenty-one, there was no way he could stop her from doing it. Quickly realizing that she was right, Bernhard had attempted to compromise, offering to hire a companion who would travel with her, but Cecilia had only laughed and insisted she would be fine. As an afterthought, she had added somewhat flippantly that his business needed the money more than she did.

It was that final impertinence, which Cecilia had not truly meant, that brought on her mother's anger and sparked one of the rare instances of temper that Cecilia could remember. With a raised voice and trembling finger, Camille had admonished her daughter for disrespect and disobedience, calling her an ungrateful brat and demanding she apologize to her father. Cecilia had become incensed as well, and she had savored a thought which she did not speak: how she would have loved to hear her mother take such a forceful tone with someone White. Still, she had apologized once her mother was on the verge of angry tears. But she had not softened her stand on traveling to America. She *would* do that, and she would do it by herself.

When her ship docked in Boston harbor several weeks later, she wondered if her father had not hired a bodyguard anyway. Had someone been following her, watching over her during the voyage? She never knew, and no one had followed her after she disembarked, so she had put the notion out of her head and concentrated on her business.

She had intended to do more than drop into the solicitor's office and sign papers after she arrived in the city. This would be her only chance to get to know her grandparents, and so she had planned on staying a while in the house and combing through all of its contents. When she had stopped at the executor's law office to retrieve the keys, she had met the handsome junior attorney handling her grandparents' affairs. She had been surprised to see that he was only a few years older than she was, and they had set a date and time for him to come to the house, sit down with her, and go over the will in its entirety.

That day was today, and as Cecilia looked out through the open window, she knew she could examine the house contents much more attentively if she did not have to worry about someone jumping out from behind a door while her back was turned.

The constable sat behind his desk politely listening and gazing at her with undisguised curiosity. Cecilia had heard that in this country, the constables and bobbies preferred to be called *coppers*, and she knew as she spoke that this one was trying to determine her race. She feared his resolve to act might lessen if he decided she was something other than an exotic European, so she spoke quickly—laying her accent on as heavily as she could—and ended by asking if someone could check on her that evening. To her great relief, he promised to leave word for the night watch, and he offered to send someone by that afternoon to walk through the house with her. The two of them together could then make sure there were no squatters or miscreants hiding in its untended reaches.

Once that bit of business was done, she hurried back to Beckley Street to keep her appointment with the solicitor.

J. M. Philbert rang the bell at twenty minutes after one in the afternoon.

She held the door for him and then led him to the parlor where she invited him to sit while she prepared a pot of tea. When she returned with a silver tea tray, she poured them each a cup, and then she gave him an account of the strange goings-on of the past week.

"It would not surprise me," Philbert said after several moments of deep thought, "to learn that the poor souls are reaching out to you in the only way they can."

"Doubtful," Cecilia said immediately and with an indulgent smile. "Such things only happen in books, and in the fevered imaginations of the unenlightened. Why would they pound on the walls and act as if they intended to wreck the place? I'm surprised to hear a man of letters say such a thing."

"The world is strange," Philbert replied, sipping his tea. "There are more things in heaven and earth than are dreamt of in our philosophies." He paused and then added, "May the Bard forgive my presumptiveness."

Cecilia continued to smile as she gazed into her cup.

"With due regard to Mister Shakespeare," she said, "I think it much more likely a troublemaker has determined to frighten me away. Obviously, someone wishes to have their way with my grandparents' legacy. Perhaps someone was even hired by another who wishes to own this property and would do anything to acquire it. Especially if I might be frightened into selling it for mere pence."

"Ah, but if that is true, how does one explain a door which opens by itself and reveals no one on its other side?"

"There are ways," she said. "Mesmerists and magicians command all manner of unnatural occurrences, even when standing before a large audience on a lighted stage. Imagine what one might do in a darkened house. Although, I suppose it would be much less trouble to simply burn the place down with me in it."

"Don't say such things!" Philbert snapped with sudden earnestness. He set his cup aside. "A woman such as you may invite trouble unwittingly."

She tilted her head. "A woman such as me, Mr. Philbert?"

He coughed, flustered, and looked away from her. "A very beautiful woman, alone and unprotected. Such exquisite, surpassing beauty…if you will pardon my boldness in saying so."

He coughed into his fist again and flushed, embarrassed by the candor of his words.

Cecilia blushed from collar to hairline. She cast her eyes about the room as if she had never seen it before, and neither of them spoke until Philbert coughed once more and reached into his valise for a hefty, double ring of keys and a sheaf of papers.

He read every page of the will and apprised her of the assets she now owned. The textile mill had already been seized for taxes, but they had left her the house with all its furnishings, two carriages that she intended to sell, and a second, small plot of land outside the city. There was a small sum of money to cover the remaining estate taxes and legal fees, but it would also cover her living expenses for a while if she used it judiciously.

"I thought there would be more," she said when he was finished. "Heaven forgive me if I sound ungrateful, and I do not mean that I would feel more fortunate. It's only…if all my father told me was true—and I can think of no reason why it would not be—even without the value of the mill, there should be a great deal more."

"Ten, fifteen years ago perhaps," Philbert said. "Your grandfather's business fell into steep decline after the war. Newer methods of production, industrial automation, progress essentially, began to undermine his factory's output, but he refused to consider newer ways of doing things. He even turned away immigrants and dispossessed Whites from the South when they came looking for work because he preferred to have Negros. He was able to pay them far lower wages of course, but in time, even those savings were eaten away by the steady shrinkage of his customer base. He chose to let himself fall behind, and he paid for his hubris by losing most of what he had accumulated. This house, I'm afraid, is the most valuable thing you own, and it is obviously in need of repair if it creaks and groans the way you described."

Cecilia sighed and looked at the ceiling. "Well," she said, "I am grateful, nonetheless. There is no such thing as a bad inheritance."

"Quite right," Philbert said and handed her the rings of keys.

They talked for a half-hour more before she saw him out, going as far as the front porch to bid him farewell. Philbert took her hand with marked gentleness and kissed the back of it. He told her she was welcomed at his office or that she could send a message to the boarding house where he lived at any hour of the day or night if she had a question or needed help with anything at all. Looking into his eyes, Cecilia could easily see that he hoped she would call and was furtively inviting her to do so. She did not wish to give him a false impression, but she was deeply flattered by his attention, and so she promised to visit him before week's end and tell him when she planned to set sail for England.

A broad smile crossed Philbert's face as he turned and started down the front steps. He turned at the gate and tipped his hat again, then he walked on up the street. Cecilia suppressed her own smile until he was out of sight, then she went back into the house and closed the door.

The metal rings that held the keys were substantial by themselves, but the added heft of the metal shafts made them drag her hand down like a weight. The keys all looked alike but one, a long fat shaft with a rusted pin that poked up like the tip of a decrepit finger.

She took them all and climbed to the attic, starting there and working her way down room-by-room and floor-by-floor, searching for an oversized lock that the key would fit and wondering when the copper would arrive to search the house with her. Not that she needed him, she told herself when she had arrived back on the ground floor. She had gone through nearly the entire place and seen nothing that was out of the ordinary. There were trunks of old clothes and odd furnishings, dust-covered paintings, books, an old spinning wheel and a great deal of assorted bric-a-brac, which one would expect to find in any old house. The only places she had yet to examine were the basement and the old root cellar beneath the back window.

She decided to wait before going into the basement, but the root cellar she could certainly check, especially since it was still light out.

She found a slip of paper and wrote a note: *I am out back in the root cellar.* She affixed it to the front door, then she went down the main hallway to the kitchen and out onto the back porch.

The grass was knee-high and urgently in need of mowing. She wondered if there were snakes hiding among the tall blades.

She gathered the folds of her dress and went down the steps. The vegetation felt lush and springy beneath her shoes. She hoped she would not discover what lay hidden in the grass by having it scamper or slither up her leg.

The doors of the root cellar had been white at some point. Paint flaked from their surfaces, and a massive, rusty chain had been snaked through a pair of holes drilled above the handles, keeping them tightly closed. Trails of rust stained the gray wood like long trails of dried blood.

Cecilia looked at the faded doors, at the rusted chain, and at the iron lock that bound them closed. It was as large as both her hands together. The question of where the odd key on her ring fit was answered. It and this lock made an ugly, bloated pair, and together they should be used to lock up something that ought never to be seen under the sun again.

What could be down there that required such safeguarding?

The doors were on a slant, and Cecilia had to lean forward and prop one foot against them to reach the lock. It was heavy, and she had trouble moving it with one hand. She swung the mass of keys forward and let the chain trap them against the wood, then she grabbed the lock with her other hand and placed her other foot against the doors as well. Imagining she looked comical, and realizing she would not be able to open the doors even if they were not chained because she was standing on them, she adjusted her grip and gave the lock a strong tug anyway.

It was cold and grainy against her palms.

She let it go and straightened.

Her hands were coated with rust, and she felt slime on her fingertips. That must have come from some creature hiding on the lock's underside. She wiped them on her dress and reached for the ring of keys, dragging them to her and taking the great key in her hand.

It was a gnarled, iron finger with dapples of rust along its length.

She leaned forward again and fitted the end of it into the lock. When nothing happened, she grasped the lock with her left hand and steadied it as best she could, then she jiggled the key and moved it back and forth in the hole. She turned it this way and that for several minutes, fighting against the weight of the other keys as she did so. The lock remained as tightly closed as her own teeth would have had she poked at them with a dried noodle.

It needed oiling, she decided.

Her arms had begun to ache, so she stopped and stood upright again, groaning at a muscle spasm in the small of her back. She stretched and thought how nice a warm bath would feel at that moment. There ought to be oil of some sort in the basement, but the thought of tripping among the old chests and boxes and the dust and spiders and mice (for there were bound to be more there than there had been in the attic) put her off. She decided to stand by her decision and wait for the copper before going down. Maybe he would find it for her and help her get this lock open. Then she told herself no; she could wait to search the basement but, in the meantime, she would deal with the lock herself.

She walked across the yard again and went back into the kitchen. In the larder, she found a chunk of fat, which she dumped into a skillet and carried to the stove. She lit a fire in the stove's cast-iron belly and set the pan on top of it. The fat began to sizzle before long, and it soon produced a pool of grease, which Cecilia carefully drained into a teacup. She carried the cup out the back door, down the steps, and across the yard to the door of the root cellar where, leaning over the lock, she carefully poured the grease into the keyhole until it overflowed and ran down the lock's rusted face. She doubted it would help, but it cost her nothing to try.

She took the teacup back and retrieved the ring of keys, pausing to wrestle with it for several minutes in hopes of getting the large key free. It was no use. Her hands were too small, and she was not strong enough to open the ring and free the one she wanted from the mass of other keys. She sighed and took the entire bunch back out to the cellar doors.

The sun would set before long. It hovered in the treetops and sent long shadows across the yard. How much time had she spent going through the upper floors of the house after Philbert departed? Undoubtedly more than she had intended if the afternoon was gone already, and evening was approaching.

She braced her foot against the doors a final time and stuck the key into the lock. She adjusted her grip and gave it several hard turns.

The lock protested and held firm at first. She flexed the fingers of her right hand and tried again. The lock fought, but she jiggled the key and felt the tiniest slip after several more twists of her arm. She went on digging the key into the mechanism, then the rusted arm popped open, and the iron bulk slid to one side.

The abrupt movement and the sudden, heavy rattle of the chain startled her so that she drew back and almost tumbled into the grass. A strange sensation passed through her like an arrow piercing her body. For a split second she saw a woman dressed head-to-toe in black, kneeling not a foot away from her, a Bible clutched in her hands and a crucifix on the ground in front of the cellar doors. The vision was gone the next instant, but in its place was an indefinable sense that the world had shifted just now. The lock and chain still held, having moved only a few inches after all, but they now seemed compromised, less sturdy than when she had first come out to look at them. Powerful and forbidding before, they were now just rusted metal.

Cecilia looked around the yard, her flesh beginning to crawl as she did so. She reminded herself that she was not Camille Blessington; she was not afraid of shadows. But as her eyes took in the lengths of darkness growing across the grass and her ears the mocking squawk of a crow, she did feel afraid: more afraid, even, than she had felt in her bedroom on the previous nights.

It was nine o'clock when she heard a loud rapping at the door. The sound startled her and caused the book she was holding to tumble out of her hands. The house was winning; it was eroding her courage and turning her into the very sort of woman she had always looked down on. She might have to book passage back to England and leave everything in the solicitor's hands.

She picked up the oil lamp and went into the front hallway where she undid the bolt and pulled the front door open a crack. She half expected to see Mr. Philbert, but a night watchman lifted his lantern and touched the brim of his cap with a finger. The glittering buttons on his tunic reassured her, so she opened the door all the way and invited him in.

"Good evening Madam," he said. "The Watch Commander has given orders for a close observance of these premises tonight. Had some trouble have you?"

Cecilia asked him to sit but he refused, so she talked to him briefly about the noises she had heard over the past week and the open window she had found early that very morning. She told him about her visit to the station, about how she had searched the house while waiting for a copper to stop by that afternoon, and about finding nothing out of the ordinary. She was convinced someone was trying to scare her away.

The watchman listened with interest. When she was done, he told her he would check the yard and then circle back in an hour as he made his rounds. In the meantime, if something out of the ordinary happened she should stick her head out an upstairs window and call at the top of her lungs to arouse the neighbors.

Cecilia thanked him, feeling a sudden, renewed sense of calm. She smiled and shut the door as he stepped off the porch; then she lifted her lamp and went back into the parlor. After another hour of reading, she confidently blew out the lamp and made her way upstairs to her room. She said her prayers, undressed, and crawled into bed. In no time at all, she was fast asleep.

Hours into the night, she heard an iron bar clang against the hearthstones in the kitchen. She groaned and turned over, listening against her will to that and a torrent of other sounds that came up through the floor. When a porcelain vase shattered against the wall in the parlor, she sat up and reached for the candle. Her fingers clutched it then she hesitated. Another large piece of porcelain crashed against a downstairs wall. She flung off the covers and got to her feet, her anger mounting as she rummaged in the dark for a match.

She had had enough.

If someone wanted her out, they would have to take her by the neck and throw her out. She would not let fear rule her and make her spend her nights shivering under a blanket while hooligans violated what now belonged to her.

She would not stand for it. Whatever happened, she would not stand for this.

The wick sputtered to life but nearly died a moment later when she snatched the candle up and spun toward the door. She marched across the room, grasped the loose knob and yanked it with all her might, enraged at the sounds. The knob came off in her hand and she hurled it against the door with a shout of fury and indignation. It thumped against the wood and clunked loudly to the floor where it rolled in a circle at her feet.

A solid thump answered from downstairs.

There was a moment of total silence, then she felt a second thump through the soles of her feet. She stooped and picked up the doorknob.

Setting the candle on the floor, she knelt at the door and tried to slide the knob back onto the spindle. It pushed against the metal bar and threatened to send the outside knob falling to the floor as well. She grabbed the spindle with her fingers and drew it back, holding it while she tried to fit the knob back on. A sudden, rhythmic creaking from downstairs made her stop.

Someone was walking.

As she listened, the flat, heavy footfalls made their way to the bottom of the staircase and stopped. A booming thud came up through the floor, as if something gargantuan had reached up and pounded its fist against the boards of the ceiling.

She stood and looked over her shoulder at the window.

Would the watchman hear her if she called? Would anyone? It was far into the night. If he were like many, he might have found an out-of-the-way spot and gone to sleep by now. Would the neighbors hear her? Would they come?

The weighty footfalls started upwards. Something of an ungodly weight. She thought she heard the treads of the staircase splintering as if they would give way and collapse into the basement. When the sound reached the top of the stairs and turned toward her room, Cecilia could feel the echo of its steps through the floorboards. Something heavy and metal was being dragged behind it. The steps paused outside her door.

The outer knob rattled.

Cecilia took a backward step and held the candle in front of her. In the dim light, she could see the thin finger of iron in the knob hole turn then disappear completely, pulled from the other side of the door.

She began to wheeze. She fell backward another step and heard the knob hit the floor in the hallway.

It was not a person—of that, she was sure—and what it was she could not guess, but with or without eyes, the entity in the hallway could see her. It could taste her fear, and she felt for the first time a pitch-black malice radiating through the wood itself, reaching through the knob hole like a tendril, searching.

The candlestick slipped from her hand and clunked on the floor, snuffing the taper out in a splash of wax and a spiral of smoke. She turned and ran to the window. Pushing the curtains aside, she reached for the sash and pushed up on it with both hands.

It didn't budge.

She pushed again, straining against the wooden frame, but the window stuck as firmly as if it had been nailed shut. She turned back to find the candlestick, but it was lost in the shadows of the floor.

The world outside the window was dank and sodden. Lampposts and sidewalks glistened under rolling sheets of fog, and the glow of the gaslights coalesced into watery yellow orbs. The illusory globes of light dissipated and reformed in the waves of atmospheric moisture passing over them. Despite their presence, a shroud of darkness and menace blanketed the street and shut it off from the rest of the world. Cecilia was utterly alone: beyond the help of the neighbors, the watchman, her parents, or anyone.

More sounds of destruction came from downstairs. The door to the room began groaning as if it would fly off its hinges.

Cecilia's heart battered the inside of her chest. Fright drained her strength and slithered in the pit of her stomach like worms. She felt pressure building below her waist, then a spurt of water wet her legs before she could stop it. Tears pooled in her eyes and her throat constricted.

She had ignored safety and sensibility. She had scorned her mother's fears and bent her father to her will until he allowed her sail off to a land she had never seen like an adventurer weaned on hardship. How she had disdained her mother's reclusiveness and caution. How she had mocked the woman who gave her life and the father who wanted to protect her. She wanted their protection now, by God. By all the Saints in heaven, she would have done anything to be back with her parents now.

Disgusted and terrified, she gathered the folds of her gown and stepped away from the moisture on the floor.

More pounding. The door strained against its frame.

She ran to the farthest corner of the room and crouched behind a rocking chair, hoping it and the darkness would be enough to conceal her. A terrible clatter echoed through the walls. Something had been thrown against the upstairs banister and gone tumbling down the staircase. When the crashing stopped, she heard a second set of heavy feet start towards the upper floor.

J.M. Philbert had spent the previous afternoon and evening in agony. He had fought down the urge to go back to the house and call on her uninvited when he left his office for home. He had passed the night obsessing over the memory of her hand in his, the memory of her touch and the delicate scent that wafted from her skin when he pressed the backs of her fingers to his lips.

As he dressed for the office that morning, he made up his mind to accept whatever embarrassment he might cause her or bring upon himself by calling on her unannounced. He would not dither, nor allow nervousness to weaken his resolve. If Cecilia Blessington would consent to receive him, he would swim the Atlantic Ocean to visit her and, at the appropriate time, he would ask for that same delicate hand in marriage.

When the carriage arrived at seven to pick him up, he gave the driver the address on Beckley Street and told him to stop there before going to the office. The morning was mild and the sun was out, but it was early yet, and the streets and walkways were still damp from last night's heavy fog.

When the carriage stopped in front of Cecilia's house, Philbert was taken by a sense of...wrongness. He climbed out of the carriage, his forehead wrinkling.

"I'll be just a moment," he told the driver. The man nodded and set the reins down beside his foot.

From the street, Philbert could see that the front door was unsecured and slightly ajar. He went up the walk, climbed the steps to the porch, and tapped on the door with the head of his walking stick. There was no response, so he took off his hat and stepped into the foyer, calling as he went.

"Miss Blessington? Cecilia?"

The downstairs had been ransacked. Broken crockery and smashed figurines littered the floors. In the front hallway, a broken table leaned against the wall at the foot of the stairs, and a gaping hole yawned in the wall above its wreckage.

"Miss Blessington?" he called again as he followed the trail of destruction through to the kitchen and the rear door, which stood completely open. He went out onto the back porch, and his eyes were drawn to the doors of the root cellar at the corner of the house. The doors were battered and hung off their hinges at a bazaar angle as if ripped open by a terrible wind.

He climbed off the porch and walked across the untended grass to the entrance of the shadowy hole that stretched out of sight beneath the house. The rickety steps that went down into its recesses were covered with fibrous clods of red dirt and loam. He took a breath and went down the steps to the disturbed earth at their base.

In the dimness, he went as far as he dared and, in a far corner, his eyes made out the remains of a shallow pit. In the mound of dirt beside it, even in the sparse light, he saw the ragged mixing of soil, pebbles, and bits of clothing debris. A nauseating stink hung in the air and threatened his stomach.

It was an opened grave.

He pulled out his handkerchief and covered his mouth and nose as he backed toward the steps. *Dear God... What is this?*

He hurried back into the house and retraced his steps through the destroyed kitchen. He crossed the parlor a second time and stopped at the foot of the staircase.

Erratic markings defaced the walls. Root fibers and clumps of dirt marred the treads of the staircase while shattered spindles hung between the steps and the balustrade like broken teeth. His eyes followed the destruction upward until the stairs reached the landing and turned out of sight.

Taking the loose handrail, he started up.

"Cecilia?"

Every door on the second floor was closed except one halfway down the hall. Marred and splintered, it spilled light into the hallway and beckoned him in silence.

He walked to the door, placed a shaking hand against its face and pushed.

"Cecilia?"

She was in her nightgown, sitting motionless in a rocking chair in the corner, illuminated by sunlight that came in through the opened curtains.

Her head moved when he said her name. Slowly, stiffly, it turned as if it were balanced atop her body but unattached, and it stopped when her vacant eyes found him.

Philbert's jaw dropped.

Her face was ashen and creased, her brown eyes fogged with cataracts as if she were more than a century old. He moved into the room.

"Cecilia?"

The cloying odor of illness and rot permeated the air. He went to the window and tried to raise it but it would not budge. He took a deep breath through his handkerchief and went to the chair.

"What's happened to you?" he asked as he knelt. "Have you sent for the police?"

She stood suddenly and Philbert flinched.

"I-I shall send for a doctor," he said, stumbling to his feet and collecting himself.

The whites of her eyes were bloodshot and spotted. Deep lines and crow's feet creased the skin around their sockets like cracks in a plaster mask.

The smell threatened his stomach again.

She raised a hand to her head and pulled the slumber cap off, freeing a mass of graying hair and dropping the cap to the floor. Philbert noted the large stains on the front of her gown.

Cecilia dear, what has happened to you?

As he watched, she took the front of the gown in her hands and ripped it. Her nails were strangely thick and opaque whereas, when he had taken her hand the day before, they had been rosy pink and delicate. The fabric of her gown was tightly woven, and he would have doubted she was strong enough to tear it, but her hands made it separate as easily as a child's would have a sheet of paper.

"Cecilia!"

The gown tore from bodice to hemline and slid from her shoulders, crumpling to the floor and wreathing her feet. He averted his eyes and hurried to the bed, where he grabbed the spread by a corner and dragged it free. Taking it in both hands, he threw it around her, embracing her though he was repelled by her eyes and by the smell that poisoned the air in the room.

She put her head back and screamed when his arms closed around her, then she flung him off with incredible strength. The sound of her scream was unnaturally loud, deafening as a ship's whistle, piercing as the scream of someone plunging to her death. It seemed to rattle the windows, and Philbert clapped his hands over his ears, wincing and feeling his teeth vibrate.

Her head swiveled until the dead eyes found him, then she was on him in an instant, locking her fingers into his hair and turning to drag him toward the bed. Fire sluiced over Philbert's scalp, and he thought the very skin of his head was being torn from his skull. He bellowed in pain and seized the grotesque hand in both of his, trying to force the fingers open and free himself from the awful grip.

She was monstrously strong.

He struggled to his feet, fighting her, desperate to get her fingers unwound. She let go suddenly but grabbed him with the other hand and wrapped her fingers around his throat. Her grip was so fierce, it forced him onto his toes even though he was taller, and he hung off her hand like an oversized doll.

He panicked.

Lashing at the distorted face with both fists, he struck her repeatedly, and when that proved useless, he grabbed her head with both hands and twisted as hard as he could. Though he felt he had grabbed a handful of stone, he twisted until the tendons in her neck threatened to rip apart and tear through her skin. Still, she held him until he was on the verge of blacking out. Then she let him go and he dropped to the floor in a heap.

He gasped for air and crawled away from her. There was a metal candlestick half-hidden under the edge of the bed. He lunged for it. Heavy and slick with wax, it fit his hand like a club. He staggered to his feet and spun around, the stick raised above his head, ready to split her skull with its squared base.

But she was standing in the middle of the room, bent at the waist and clutching her abdomen, a thick string of yellow fluid hanging from her lips. As Philbert watched, her back arched, relaxed, and arched again in a backbreaking heave. A shiny, bloody mass of offal bulged out of her throat and dangled until it broke free and dropped to the floor.

Philbert retched.

The sight and the smell of it overwhelmed him, and his own stomach forced out its contents. He dropped the candlestick, eyes watering.

Dear God....

Cecilia fell to her knees and heaved again, her hands still clutching her belly. Blood spurted from her nose and dribbled from her mouth and chin.

Philbert pulled the top sheet off the bed. He went to her as she collapsed onto her side and fought to breathe. A wail of pain bubbled out of her, and she curled into a fetal knot. He threw the sheet over her, careful not to touch her this time. Her breathing was fast and shallow, and he could hear masses of fluid and mucus gurgling deep within her each time she inhaled. He waited on his knees, hoping the shallow, rapid breaths would slow.

The driver.

The driver would have to go and bring a doctor. Was it safe to leave her, even for the time it would take to run downstairs and send the man for help?

She sat up suddenly and got to her knees. A whimper began deep in her chest and morphed into a brittle cry. Her back arched. Strangling, gagging on something wedged in her throat; she fought to bring it up. A gristly lump finally dislodged itself and dropped from her mouth. Philbert turned his head, but he had already seen what was there, and the image would never leave him. A splash of bile and spittle twitched on the floor; in it was a tiny human hand.

He threw his arms around her and pulled her to him without thinking. Tears coursed from her eyes and soaked the creases in her skin, diluting the blood that covered the lower half of her face. As Philbert watched, the deep cracks began to smooth themselves out. He tried to wipe the blood away but only smeared it across her cheeks and chin. Beneath its scarlet tinge, traces of her true color began infusing her face.

He wrapped the sheet around her as best he could and dragged her out of the room. In the hallway, he lifted her into his arms and made his way to the top of the stairs where he again fumbled with the sheet. Drawing it up with one hand so that it would not trip him, he quickly and carefully made his way down the ruined staircase, mindful of a wet, thumping sound that had started in the bedroom above.

"God didn't like what that man did," the maid said. "There were some who did worse, surely, but God didn't like what went on inside that house. The son took that girl and ran off because he thought the living were gonna make life hard for them. He didn't know the truth. Maybe if he'd stayed, his father wouldn't have gone insane. Maybe he could have kept him from bringing that woman into the house."

J.M. Philbert didn't speak at first. He was still haunted by what he had seen in Cecilia's bedroom on that awful morning. After she was admitted to Massachusetts General, he had taken police to the house and shown them the demolished downstairs and the blood and muck-covered floor of the bedroom where the sickening remains of what she had expelled were melted into pools of liquid. When she was able to talk, the investigator listened to her story of all that had happened and decided vandals were indeed to blame. They had broken in to terrorize her and wreak havoc upon the house. That explained the noises she had heard on the nights leading up to the attack. Although they had been helpful to her early on, the police seemed to condemn her afterward. A woman who flouted society's rules, they seemed to say, opened herself up to victimization.

The extreme illness that Philbert described to the physician and other caregivers was ascribed to food poisoning. She would be fine, they told him, after a few days of rest and a liquid diet.

"I took her back to London," Philbert told the maid. "Her parents were nearly dead with worry, and when they saw her...they knew something unspeakable had happened."

The woman crossed herself.

"It must have been her grandmother's contrition that freed her from the evil," he went on. "Perhaps because she prayed for forgiveness and then left this life willingly and without struggle...perhaps her sacrifice imparted some positive force..."

"It was the good Lord," the maid said. "Best leave it at that."

Philbert nodded and let his gaze drift to the room's far corner.

"I was forced to leave them after a week," he said, "and I did so with a great deal of reluctance. She was seated in front of the fireplace, staring into the flames. Her young sister was terrified of her, even though she seemed perfectly normal again in appearance. Her parents said that they would apprise me of her condition after she had had time to recover fully, but my letters have gone unanswered, and I've heard nothing of her since."

"That poor girl," the woman said.

Silence settled at the table.

He had been desperate to figure out what happened during the terrible hours of that night, and as Cecilia would tell him nothing, he decided—after returning to the States—to look for someone who might have an answer. He could think of no better person than the woman who had found the old

Blessingtons dead, and he was fortunate to find her, for every one of the exploited Negro workers had long since moved on.

"What will become of that...place?" the woman asked.

"Her father has told me to sell it or, if no one will buy it, to tear it down. Which I think is the better answer."

"It would do the world some good," she said, still clutching the crucifix. "Please, burn that abominable place to the ground. Get rid of it once and for all."

Outside her walls, the day was waning. Night came quickly at this time of year, and Philbert was no longer comfortable being out of doors after the day ended.

He got to his feet.

"I will take my leave now," he said. He wished the woman good health and gave her money for her trouble. Outside, his breath made a cloud in the autumn air. He hailed a carriage and gave the driver his address.

"Go apace," he said as he climbed in. "I'd like to be home in time for dinner."

"As you wish," the driver replied and snapped the reins.

Philbert settled into the seat and set his valise on his lap. The streets of Beacon Hill drifted past, aglow in the umber light of dusk. When the cab took a now familiar turn onto the cobbles of Beckley Street, toward the accursed house, he pushed himself all the way back in the seat and turned his face away.

VI.
Obsidian Sky

"What do you see?" the boy asked.

The man squinted into field glasses and searched the silvery outline of the great dark spot floating above the mountains where the moon should have been. He heard fear in the boy's voice, and it tugged at his heart.

"Nothing," he said at last. "About the same as what we can see with our eyes." He lowered the binoculars and felt his son's hand slip into his own. The boy was getting too big for this, for handholding with his old man. He did it because his mother still led him around like he was five years old, because she couldn't walk across a parking lot without....

He shook his head and reminded himself to let it go.

All of it. Just let it go.

He gave the boy's hand a gentle squeeze and found the comforting effect of it ran both ways. Perhaps the woman knew something he didn't know. Right now, the child was frightened, that was all. And he had every right to be, considering.

The full moon, distended and pale, had climbed above the mountains behind the cabin an hour before the sun set. The man had busied himself chopping logs for the fireplace while the boy scampered through ankle-deep drifts of leaves wielding a hickory light saber. Now and again, the sound of chopping would cease while the man looked down at the stark beauty of the moon reflected in the lake at the foot of the hill. Mare Imbrium—the Sea of Storms—lay like a birthmark across the lunar face, and he was staring directly at it when a pinpoint of light flared at its center. He wondered if it was the glimmer of an airplane heading into the sunset, or if a meteor had flickered as it burned up in the atmosphere. In either case, it had come and gone in the space of a thought, like a flash bulb set off miles above him. Then the October sky was empty and clear again. He was not a scientist, but he knew beyond doubt that an explosion on the lunar surface—one visible from earth with the naked eye—would be one hell of an explosion indeed. Something in the hundreds of thousands (maybe even millions) of megatons.

It was ironic that he had always loved science and the cosmos, yet he had no head for math and numbers beyond what was required for high school graduation. In college, he had been forced to accept the limits of his ability, and he had turned aside from a career in the space sciences. A decade later, he earned his living writing code for computers and handheld gadgets. It wasn't cutting-edge exploration at the boundaries of human knowledge, but it allowed him to use his brain, and it brought him a degree of satisfaction many working stiffs could only wish for.

He'd gathered up an armful of the split logs for later that night, then he and the boy had gone inside for hot dogs and beans.

The cabin had running water and electricity, but he used them sparingly. He wanted to keep these outings as close to nature as he could, even knowing how the boy's mother would react if she found out he had used the outhouse or bathed in the lake: things that were good for him, but things she would never understand or approve of. When the dishes were washed and put away and the camp stove stowed for the evening, he got the fishing tackle out of its corner and made ready for the next day. While he worked, the boy amused himself with an electronic game, pausing now and then to toss a question across the room.

The man inventoried the tackle box and cleared the creel of mouse droppings, then he turned his attention to the spin-cast reels and the knots in the line his son would use. He was fixated on the task when it occurred to him the world outside had grown incredibly dark.

The sun had already settled behind the trees when they'd come in, and it must be well below the horizon by now, but the moon was full, so the outside world should not have looked like the bottom of a well at midnight. Not so soon, anyway.

He reached out and lowered the flame of the kerosene lamp in the center of the table. A hint of fire, ghostly and blue, lingered in the glass chimney, dancing above the ember of the wick while the cabin's interior plunged into primordial darkness.

"Dad?" the boy said.

Hearing the uncertainty in his son's voice, he turned the flame up again.

He rose from the table and walked across the room to the door. The boy did not move from his spot in front of the cold fireplace.

"It sure got dark in a hurry," the child said.

"Yeah," the man answered.

He could see nothing, so he pushed the screen door open and stepped onto the creaking planks of the porch.

Black as a cave, he thought.

New moon black. Blacker even.

The orange light from inside the cabin was weak beyond the doorway. It spilled across the threshold in a barely visible oblong but, if he could see it at all, it was spoiling his night vision, so he reached back and pulled the door closed.

He shut his eyes and counted to sixty.

When he opened them again, he was no longer floating in a bottle of ink, but it was still much too dark. The Bortle Dark Sky rating for the area around the lake normally equaled Class 3 or 4, darkness that required a flashlight outdoors but was perfectly suitable for stargazing. What he saw around him now was Class 2, perhaps even Class 1 darkness—the darkness seen in the most remote regions of Australia and central Asia, the Peruvian mountains, or the Congo. Areas that were hundreds of miles from any city.

He went to the edge of the porch and looked up, wondering if a blanket of cloud had moved in and snuffed out what remained of the evening's illumination. The sky was clear, and an impossible number of stars swirled above the valley. He stepped down into the leaves and walked away from the cabin, turning as he went, looking back at the mountains buttressing the sky on the far side of the lake.

What he saw astounded him.

The mountain range was backlit by a thread of aquamarine light, and high above it, the Milky Way glittered like a trove of diamonds hurled against the night sky. A sphere of utter darkness floated against the chaos of celestial lights—a black hole at the center of his vision. The globe of the moon was gone, and in its place was an obsidian disc silhouetted by the rampant starlight.

"Jesus Christ..."

Nothing stirred—not a cricket, not an owl. Neither a frog nor a single fly disturbed the silence. Even the wind off the lake had ceased rattling the autumn leaves.

He swallowed and called to the boy.

"Jeremy!"

His voice jarred the stillness and broke its hold for just a moment. Then the quiet rushed back with oppressive vengeance.

The screen door squeaked open.

"Yeah Dad?"

"Bring my binoculars, will you?"

A minute later, the door screeched again then banged shut as the boy ran through it and leaped off the porch. He took two steps in the crackling leaves and stopped.

"Dad?"

"I'm right here."

He could see clearly in the starlight now, but their unaccustomed brightness gave an eerie look and feel to the landscape. Waiting for his son to cross the yard, he felt the unease that lingered on the margins of his imagination and stirred whenever he found himself without light in an unfamiliar place. It was childish, the fear that prodded him, and he resented its persistence; but here again it came skulking along the edge of his mind, looking to take over his thoughts. Their fort, their clubhouse, turned into a lonely hovel in the dark woods, and there wasn't a soul with whom they could commiserate for a mile in any direction.

"Come look," he said, clearing his throat and forcing his voice to remain level. Maybe he could preserve the atmosphere of discovery and adventure. God forbid the boy should find out how scared he himself was.

"It's too dark to see anything," the boy said, coming to stand beside him.

"Not if you look up."

The boy put his head back and turned in a slow circle, stopping when his eyes fell on the dark orb of the moon. He put out a fumbling hand and grasped his father's shirttail...

The man gave his son's hand a squeeze then put an arm around the boy's shoulder.

"Can't make out anything," he said and wondered if he should say more. He knew that if he went to the truck and clicked on the radio, the words *government scientists*, *the President*, and NASA would all leap out at him, but he doubted he would learn anything useful. The part of his mind that was still calm wanted to believe there was someone somewhere who already knew what had happened and could explain what they were seeing. But it was hard to feel certain about anything with the universe turning itself inside-out before his very eyes.

"Ar-are we gonna be okay?" the boy asked.

The man patted his shoulder again.

"We're gonna be okay," he said with a confidence he did not feel.

"Dad?"

"Yeah?"

The boy paused.

"Wo-ould you mind if we go fishing another time?"

The woman would be a mass of nerves, he knew, and she would be livid because his phone was turned off, and he had taken the boy's and locked it in the glove box as soon as they pulled up to the cabin.

"I guess we could do that," the man said. "And anyway, your mom's gonna need somebody brave to help her stay calm."

"Ronnie will," the boy said helpfully.

The man closed his eyes. The air went out of him and his abdomen constricted to the point of pain. Thankful for the darkness, he accepted the truth of what the boy had said, and then he told himself, again, to let it all go. She was his wife, and this was his son, but the process of fading was already underway. He had already lost one, and as the years moved on, he would lose them both. The gap would widen as his son grew older, and in time, their life together would recede to nothing more than a place in memory where something good had happened long ago. And when that day came, he would become as invisible as the obsidian moon floating in the darkened sky.

He had intended to stay awake the entire night.

There was nothing he could do about what they had seen, but life seemed tenuous now, and he was reluctant to loosen his grip on it by going to sleep. When he opened his eyes at the crack of dawn, a thin blue light filtered through the seams around the door.

The boy slumbered in the down-stuffed bag next to the fireplace, a string of saliva visible along his cheek where it had hardened during the night. The man got up and dressed, placed a fresh log in the inner hearth and set a match to the wad of paper and kindling beneath it. Fire bloomed in the stone enclosure, and he warmed his hands and face.

The boy stirred.

There were no sounds in the cabin except the snap of flames finishing off the kindling and laying into the chunk of wood on the grate.

He stood up and went to the door, which he then opened with care. He looked back at the boy, saw he had not moved again, and eased the screen door open so that he could slip outside.

Blue sky greeted him, cloudless and chilly. His breath frosted in the still air, and he stepped off the porch to look at the mountains across the lake. A wood finch twittered in the boughs above the roof.

What a magnificent sound, he thought. After the disappearance of the lake fauna last night, he was relieved to know that he himself was not the only thing alive.

He walked up the driveway and turned to look back at the cabin again. The mountains were still there, as was the lake and all the trees.

What had he expected?

After last night, anything. Anything was possible.

This morning, however, the sky was blue, and the ground was solidly beneath his feet. Had he imagined it? Had they both? The idea seemed as impossible as the very thing he thought he had witnessed. That they would somehow share the same incredible delusion: that of a disappearing moon. Just as likely they would see Godzilla climb out of the lake and set the shore on fire with his breath.

He caught the smell of smoke at that instant.

A thin curl of bluish gray hovered above the chimney.

The boy would be hungry when he woke up. He was always hungry, which was a good thing. It meant he wasn't sick, and he was growing. There was cereal and bread in the larder, and he'd gotten milk when they'd stopped in town yesterday. That would certainly hold them for an hour or two, but it might prove easier and more beneficial to load up the SUV and stop at McDonald's on the edge of the town. They would have to go that way to get to the Interstate anyhow, and the boy's first thought (after food) would probably be about his mother.

The man shook his head and imagined her ire when she finally did get them on the phone.

He sighed.

Whatever they were going to do, they might as well get started. He went to the truck and opened his door. Maybe there was something useful on the radio now. He fished in his pocket, then he checked the ignition.

The keys were still inside the cabin.

He pushed the door closed and savored the loud *thunk* that broke the silence. Something else that was normal on this first day of a strange new age.

When he went back into the cabin, the boy was awake, lying on his back and staring at the ceiling. He didn't speak.

"Hungry?" the man asked.

"Nah. Not really."

"Well that's unusual."

The boy shrugged.

"We better pack up and get going," the man said. "Mom's gonna be worried."

The boy pushed himself into a sitting position.

"Is the sky..." he began and stopped. "Is everything like it's sup-posed to be?"

"As far as I can tell. We'll find out something when we turn the radio on. Are you sure you don't want breakfast? We can grab some cereal now, or we can stop at that McDonalds we passed on the way in."

The boy's eyes brightened.

"Okay then. Let's get moving."

"From NPR News in Washington, I'm Margaret Lin..."

It was like the day after 9-11. Or the day after the President had been shot. Every conversation was the same. Every person on earth asked the same questions; everyone waited on pins and needles while the authorities tried to figure out what was going on.

"The head of the International Astronomical Union has said that there is no known precedent for the event that caused the moon to lose all reflectivity twelve hours ago. Millions of people in North and South America and across the Pacific witnessed a flash on the lunar surface that was followed by the total darkening of Earth's natural satellite. Astronomers around the world continue to investigate the event in an attempt to piece together an explanation. Some believe the obvious cause of the flash was an impact by a massive asteroid, but there is still no explanation for the darkness that followed. The President will address the nation from the Oval Office at eight o'clock this evening..."

The cabin and the lake were four miles outside the nearest town. The town itself was ninety miles north of the city.

Listening to the radio, he drove the two-lane thread of Route 8 until it passed the Corwin's Crossing town limit and intersected with Main Street. They passed a church whose doors stood wide open as congregants crowded inside. A block away, the High Horse Bar & Grill was also open, and judging from the number of cars in the parking lot, it too was full. People along the sidewalks watched him drive through, nodding when they made eye contact. The boy sat in the back seat and played with his game.

The restaurant was busy for a small town. While workers moved back and forth in the kitchen area, two girls at the counter took orders with a bored precision that came from years of grinding practice and repetition.

A twenty-something man dressed in hunter's camouflage pushed back his John Deere cap and leaned on the counter with his forearms.

"I can switch out that manifold tomorrow if you still wanna bring it by," he said to one of the girls.

She opened the cash register and counted out ones and pennies.

"If there is a tomorrow," she said and handed him the money.

The boy's appetite came back with a vengeance. He wanted the pancake platter *and* a burrito, though he could not possibly eat both. Still, the man let him order it and got a large coffee for himself, figuring he would finish whatever was left when the boy's eyes fell back into synch with his stomach.

He checked his shirt pocket for the outdated clam-shell phone that he had retrieved from the glove box. The boy's phone, with only two numbers programmed in: his and the woman's. The call log showed seventeen attempts to get through to them since the night before.

Not calling her had been wrong. It was true she treated the boy like a porcelain doll, but she had a right to be worried. He wondered how he would have felt if the boy had been with her when the excitement began, and it had been he who was not able to get in touch.

No good regretting it now. Done was done.

As he fingered the phone, it rang.

The boy froze with the burrito poised at his opened mouth.

The man checked the display even though he knew what he would see.

It was her.

Looking into his son's eyes, he flipped the phone open.

"Hello..."

A shout came from the earpiece.

"Where the *hell* is my son! *What's the matter with you? Bring him home, right now!* Do you understand? Now! And he is never going anywhere with you—"

He closed it.

The boy stared at him.

He smiled and said, "Be right back."

He got up from the table and went out the side door, where he stopped in front of a large window bearing the six-foot logo.

He called her back.

This time she positively screamed. He held the phone away from his ear until she paused, then he quickly swung the mouthpiece down to his lips.

"I'm sorry," he said. "I wasn't trying to worry you. He was scared and there was nothing we could do anyway, so I tried to keep his mind off it."

"How in the hell were you going to keep his mind off of it? Do you realize what's happening?" She fumed. "What...I just don't understand what you could be thinking. *It's the fucking moon!* How are you going to take his mind off that?"

He sighed into the phone.

"I said I'm sorry, okay? We're on our way back. If—"

"Where is he?"

"He's eating."

"Eating *where?*"

He sighed again.

"You know what?" she said, "forget it. Just bring him home. Bring my son home. You are *never*—"

He hung up.

He had to let it all go. But he also had to take it.

Things were bad, but not as bad as they could get. There was tension, but there was also a functional civility, usually, and it was only possible because they had left the lawyers out of it. If he put his foot down, if he told her what he truly thought when she had these tantrums, she would bring in the lawyers. And then things would really get bad.

The boy watched him through the window; he smiled and gave a thumbs-up.

DAYS OF UNEASE

"From NPR News in Washington, I'm Jack Woods..."

The city rose up out of the landscape in front of them. The downtown skyscrapers were Lego bricks on the horizon, obscured by the blue haze of atmosphere and distance.

"There has been a change in the condition of Earth's satellite. The Moscow Observatory, the official astronomical agency of the Russian government, now reports that Earth's moon is no longer there. An NPR correspondent at the IAU in London has been standing by."

A new voice came on.

"Scientists at the Moscow Observatory noticed a second occurrence at around three a.m. Greenwich mean time. The moon, which was struck by a massive asteroid while over the western coast of North America, lost all reflectivity after the impact. While scientists everywhere have raced to understand what is happening, the moon has continued to undergo a metamorphosis. Scientists now say that it is completely gone. Whereas previously, the moon was there but no longer reflecting light, it has now vanished entirely."

He turned the radio off.

"Wow!" the boy said without looking up from his game. He was calm again, full of food and distracted. The fear that had seized him last night was gone.

The man drove on, considering, then he clicked the radio on again.

"... singularity the size of a softball. Again, there is no known precedent for what we are seeing. Some listeners will recall that in 1994, the comet Shoemaker-Levy 9 slammed into Jupiter and provided astronomers with their first ever real-time glimpse of solar system objects colliding. Well, that event also showed in dramatic fashion the immense forces that are unleashed when such collisions occur. The string of impacts left gargantuan dark spots in Jupiter's atmosphere, many of which were larger than the Earth itself.

"Some observers last night speculated that a cloud of dust and debris large enough to obscure the entire surface of the moon had been kicked up by the impact. Astronomers and astrophysicists point out, however, that such an explanation is unlikely given the moon's lack of atmosphere. Any dust or debris thrown up would have made the moon *more* reflective.

"Scientists' new theory does not explain the event itself, but if a singularity has opened, even a small one, it could conceivably have drawn in the moon's mass in the hours since the event began.

"What concerns experts now, Jack, is the question of what will happen if a small black hole has indeed opened near the Earth. This is Amanda Beche in London."

The original voice came back.

"A number of people around the globe, some of them high government officials, have begun to ask seriously if an extraterrestrial intelligence might have played a role in last night's event..."

He turned the radio off again.

"What's a singularity?" the boy asked.

"Didn't you hear what they said just now?"

"Yep. But I still don't know what it is."

"It's a black hole."

"Like a real black hole?"

"What do you mean 'like' a real black hole?" the man asked.

"Is it like the ones that gobble up stars?"

The man sighed. "Afraid so."

"Is it gonna swallow the sun?"

"I don't know," the man said and sighed again. "I hope not."

The tunnel leading into downtown was blocked off. As he crept toward the detour, he lowered the window and tried to ask a police officer what had happened.

"Let's keep moving," the cop said without emotion or inflection. He waved the SUV into the turnoff lane.

They would have to take the Loop and go south of town, then circle back to reach the row house where she now lived. Cutting through mid-town would have saved him almost an hour, but as he drove, he found himself feeling relieved at the delay. The more he thought about what was to come, the more reluctance he felt about going anywhere near the woman.

He knew she would open the door and take the boy inside without a word to him. And when he called tonight, and tomorrow, she would let the phone ring without answering. Much as he had done. The difference was she didn't have to drive to his place and drop the boy off. She would have him for the duration, and it was he, the man, who would have to come back eventually and beg if he wanted to see his son again.

After thirty minutes, the highway angled up, and he pressed on the accelerator to maintain his speed. When they topped the rise, he slammed on the brakes, pitching the boy forward against the seatbelt. The electronic game flew over the seatback and bounced off the dashboard. A river of cars and people blocked the highway. He could suddenly see a man standing on the shoulder waving his hands above his head, trying to get him and the cars behind him to slow down. How had he missed that? There were scores of brake lights and fender-benders right in front of him, but farther down the highway, a billowing column of black smoke snaked up to the sky like a lazy, gangrenous serpent climbing an invisible trellis.

"You okay?" he asked over his shoulder.

The boy was fitting himself back into the seat and readjusting the belt.

"What happened?"

He couldn't see much: just the highway, the cars, and the pillar of soot darkening the sky.

"Don't know," he said.

He turned the radio on.

A talk show (discussing what else?) but nothing about the accident. He hit a button and the radio began flipping through stations. It went through the entire dial, but he heard nothing useful.

He put the truck in park and turned off the engine.

"Looks like we have to sit for a while," he said.

The boy yawned.

"Can we get out?" he asked.

"Probably not smart," the man replied. "Never know when the traffic will start moving again."

"Can I take my seatbelt off?"

"Okay. But the instant we move, you buckle up again."

He heard a metallic click, and then the boy was leaning over the seat, a hand on his father's shoulder.

"Wh-what do you think it is?"

"Wish I knew," the man said with a shake of his head.

"I bet Mom thinks we're never gonna come back."

"I'll bet she does too," the man said and felt another stone drop into the pit of his stomach.

He heard the distant beating of helicopter blades, then he saw not one but two of them hover into view above the dammed river of cars. As he watched them, two dots balancing on the air far ahead above the smoke...*Boom!*

It was muffled, but it was close by and unmistakable. The truck rocked on its springs and a squall of leaves and small branches rained down around it. A black mushroom appeared above the trees to his left.

What the hell...?

People who had stayed put in the surrounding vehicles began climbing out. One of the helicopters peeled away from the smoke in the distance and, like a curious housefly, darted back toward them. Something had exploded beyond the trees on the northbound side of the highway.

"What was that!"

He couldn't tell which was stronger in the boy's voice this time, worry or excitement, and he wanted to protect the child from yet another piece of disastrous news. But what was the use?

"Sounds like a car exploded," he said.

"Wow!" the boy exclaimed. "Everything is crazy today!"

You have no idea, the man thought.

"Can we get out now?"

He gave it more thought, and then he said, "Okay. Here's what we'll do. We're gonna get out and see what we can see. I'll give you a boost onto the top of the truck, then I'll climb up too."

"Cool!" the boy said and lunged for the door.

They watched the car across the highway burn from their seat atop the SUV. The helicopters buzzed overhead, and a chorus of sirens added to the cacophony of anxious noises.

"Does Mom know what's happening?" the boy asked.

"What do you mean?"

"I mean about the moon and everything."

"She knows," the man said.

"Dad?"

"Yeah?"

"I have to go to the bathroom."

They had been stuck here for over an hour. He guessed it was time for nature to come calling. A thick band of trees separated them from the north side of the interstate, but that was probably not the best place to be right now. A scattering of pines along a high embankment on the right side of the highway offered less privacy than he would have liked, but they would have to do.

He climbed down and helped the boy to the ground, then he hit the lock button on the key fob, and they started toward the shoulder of the road.

The front page of a newspaper came sliding along the asphalt, carried by a puff of wind. The boy stomped on it with his foot.

"Let me see that," the man said as he swung one leg then the other over the metal guardrail.

The boy picked it up and handed it to him, then he clambered over the railing himself, resisting his father's help.

It was the front page of the local early edition, which someone had already discarded. Beneath the screaming headline were dense columns of print that he knew would be useless in terms of information. Hours earlier, when this thing had been printed, there were still only questions and stunned reactions. A curious title below the fold caught his eye.

"*Nobel Scientist Concedes Event Could Be Caused by Extraterrestrials*," he read aloud. "*Suggests Experiment Might Have Gone Awry.*"

Further down, in a sidebar, he read, "*Calls LGM Talk 'Silly,' But Says Odds of Other Intelligences Very High.*"

"What's LGM?" the boy called without looking back as he climbed the slope.

The man folded the paper, stuffed it into his hip pocket, and turned his attention back to climbing the small hill.

"It stands for Little Green Men. Whoever wrote that is talking about ET's and aliens like the ones in the movies."

"How come it's silly?"

"Well...there's probably other life out there in space, but Greys, and Greens, and Martians with antennas and flying saucers...all that stuff is nonsense."

"Why?"

"Because if aliens traveled all the way to Earth from where they lived, they wouldn't play hide-and-seek in the mountains, or kidnap people and try to read their minds."

"Why not?"

The man exhaled and thought.

"Do you remember the time we drove all the way to Washington D.C. to see grandma?"

"Yeah."

"Took a long time to get there, didn't it?"

"Yep."

"When we got there, did we sneak around to the back of the house and watch Grandma through the windows?"

"No."

"How come?"

"'Cause that woulda been stupid."

"Why?"

"Just would have," the boy said.

When they were shielded from the highway by the slope and the thin trunks, they went to separate trees.

The man said, "After all the time we spent traveling, the smart thing to do was to ring grandma's doorbell and let her know we'd arrived. If somebody's traveled to earth from another planet or from somewhere on the other side of the galaxy, their scientists are gonna want to talk to our scientists. Don't you think?"

"What if they didn't want us to know they were here?" the boy insisted.

"Then it would be smarter for them to send probes."

"But some people say the flying saucers *are* probes."

"Yep," the man agreed. "They do say that...until some other person goes on television and swears she was abducted."

"What's that?"

"Abducted? Means kidnapped. When one person says an alien kidnapped him and took him onboard a spaceship, then others start agreeing that UFOs have pilots and crews. But, if you ask them how come the crews don't just land the ship in New York so they can find out everything they want to know, they go back to saying the crews don't want to be seen. But if the crews don't want to be seen, then they could just send out probes."

The boy thought for a moment.

"Yeah but, why didn't they just say something then? Instead of blowing up the moon?"

The man grunted. "That's a good question."

The boy zipped his pants and looked around as if he had forgotten something.

"I can't wash my hands," he said.

The man zipped his own trousers, bent down, and scooped up a batch of fallen leaves and pine needles. He crushed the vegetation between his palms and gave his hands a vigorous scrub, then he dropped the flakes and dust to the ground and brushed his hands against his jeans.

"Good as new," he said.

The boy stooped and grabbed a fistful of leaves.

"I'm calling the police," she said. "If you don't have my son at that door in the next hour, I'm calling the police."

"Go ahead," he told her. "They'll probably get to you in a day or so."

That wasn't what he had wanted to say, but he heard a male voice in the background, and the words came out before he could stop them. She went on talking, but he turned to the boy, smiled, and handed him the phone.

"Talk to your mom," he said.

"Hi, Ma!" the boy yelled as he took the phone. The shrill chatter from the other end stopped. "A car blew up!" the boy said. "It was behind some trees. And then a helicopter came...!"

The man reclined his seat and turned on the radio, searching for a jazz station this time. He found one, and he focused his thoughts on the intricate melody of the saxophone while the boy jabbered behind him.

"Nah. We're still stuck on the highway. The fire department came, but then there were *two* cars burnin' and we still couldn't move."

It was two in the afternoon.

"The newspaper said aliens blew up the moon," the boy went on. "But Dad said it wasn't aliens 'cause they woulda went to New York. Then I had to go to the bathroom. We climbed up a hill—"

He stopped.

"It's not?"

The man cocked his ear involuntarily when the boy's tone changed. On the radio, the saxophone continued.

"For real?" the boy asked. "But Dad said—"

He caught a fragment of the woman's voice despite the music.

"But Dad's smarter than some ol' scientist," the boy argued.

The man reached back and took the phone.

"What happened?" he asked.

The voice on the other end frosted over once more. The coldness came at him through the receiver, frothing like a vat of liquid helium on a table in a warm room.

"Wait," he said. "Listen. Just listen for a minute." He closed his eyes and put his other hand against his forehead. "I was wrong not to call you last night. I should have called, but I didn't. I'm sorry. Not trying to make you crazy. I just thought...well I'm not sure what I thought, but I wasn't trying to start another fight. We're stuck on the highway. The downtown tunnel was closed. Now the Loop is closed and there are cars burning on both sides of it."

"Oh my God...," she said with a tired sigh. "The mid-town tunnel is closed because eight people got killed this morning."

"Good Lord," the man said. "What happened?"

"A shooting spree..." Her voice was lifeless. "Some nut with a gun, and then somebody else trying to be a hero. They killed eight people."

He said nothing for several seconds, then...

"We're coming straight there just as soon as they open the highway. He's fine. There's just nothing else we can do right now. If Scotty *is* up there, he ought to go ahead and beam us out of this mess."

Half-hearted and ill timed, the joke evaporated like smoke, leaving no indication of its passing.

"It's not aliens," she said.

"It's not? Somebody's sure?"

"You haven't seen the news since this morning." Like her son's, her utterances were sometimes hard to classify. This one was half a declarative statement and half a question. "A black hole opened near the moon," she went on, "around the same time that the asteroid hit. CNN says it's bigger than California."

"It *is* a black hole?" he asked. "I was listening to NPR. No one was sure, and they said it was only the size of a softball."

Which meant nothing; the two events could not possibly be related.

"Maybe it got bigger," she said, cutting across his thoughts. "One person says the moon caused it; another one says it didn't. One says it's too small to swallow the moon in a few hours, another one say's it's not... I don't know."

Earth's moon was, or had been, a dead rock. There hadn't been geological activity on the moon since before the dinosaurs. But both facts were irrelevant because black holes were caused by collapsing stars. *Massive* collapsing stars. They didn't just spring into existence. At least they hadn't before last night, and in any case, it was impossible for the moon to have formed one. It just was.

"A black hole..." he muttered.

The woman started to cry.

"They say it's going to suck up the atmosphere and pull the earth apart..."

Beneath the chill of her voice had been debilitating fear, he now saw. So much time had passed since he had seen the warmer side of her. The emotional distance was a chasm now, and he didn't know what to say to comfort her.

"How long...?" he asked. Maybe if he kept her talking...

"*I don't know!*" she screamed suddenly. "I don't know! Just bring him home. Please! Bring my baby home..."

He heard the phone fall against something hard and disconnect.

"What'd she say?" the boy asked after a time.

The man thought before he spoke.

"She said it *is* a black hole."

"Wow! So what do we do now?"

He didn't know.

"I think we'll just have to wait for the highway to clear."

He started the engine at fifteen after four. The light was starting to fade.

The boy was asleep on the back seat.

He had been sitting on the guardrail talking to a retired mail carrier when someone in the milling crowd noticed movement down the highway. The fire beyond the trees had been extinguished, but the word was that at least two people had died in the explosion. A man who looked vaguely like him (from the description) had stopped his car and gotten out. He had torn off his shirt and, with a long stick, calmly worked one sleeve of it into his gas tank. Then he had set fire to the shirt and walked away.

On their own side of the highway, a tanker truck had left the road and upended. There had been ample time to walk down and see what was happening, but he had not wanted to take the boy, so he had remained on the guardrail while the boy climbed back into the rear seat and played. When the battery in the electronic game died, the boy had dug around in his backpack until he found a book, then he had lain down on the seat and read until he dozed off.

When this day had dawned, the man's chief concern had been finding out what all of humanity wanted to know. As the chilling revelations unfolded one-by-one, his concern had shifted to getting the boy under cover, getting him back to his mother even, if that was the only way to keep him safe. The line of traffic moved forward, and he felt the whole of his concentration bending in that direction. Get the boy off this highway and inside some place safe. He inched along, relieved by the light snoring that drifted up from the back seat.

The cars squeezed into one lane.

He had gone a half mile when a wide swath of blackened grass came into view beyond the flashing lights of rescue vehicles. As he drew closer to the epicenter of the accident, the asphalt changed from gray to black; the white paint of the lane divide shriveled and browned; the trunks and branches of trees close to the road were scorched and blackened as well, all signs of a huge explosion and a tremendous fire. Tow trucks sat in line and waited with lights flashing while state troopers, firefighters, men and women in Highway Safety Administration windbreakers scuttled back and forth behind yards and yards of yellow tape strung from the side mirrors and cargo bay doors of cruisers, fire trucks, and unmarked official vehicles.

He let two full car lengths open between him and the vehicle in front to lessen the likelihood of bumping if the other driver (or he himself) became distracted by the chaos and gore of the crash.

The giant, foam-covered husk of the tanker truck lay upside down in the median like a sun-blackened bug that had been spit on by a bored and irreverent child. The area around it was a field of ash and mud, and the gray-black skeletons of burned and partially burned cars were scattered nearby.

My God, he said to himself. A tickle in his brain reminded him of the car in front, and he looked up in time to see brake lights flashing frantically.

He jammed his own brakes and heard the light *plop* of the boy's book as it was propelled onto the floor. The boy stirred but did not wake up.

He raised his hand apologetically, signaling to the woman behind the wheel who glared at him in the rearview before pulling away. He took a last look at the blasted landscape, then he pulled away also.

It felt like days since they had left the cabin, yet, when he pulled off the highway fifteen minutes later, he found himself dreading the nearness of the woman's home and the short time that remained before they got there. He was starving, but he dared not stop again until he was in front of her door. The boy would be ready to eat a horse if he were awake.

Soon.

Soon it would all end. Or should he say it would begin? What would he do once the boy was safely delivered, and he had to go back to the old apartment? What would he do when he was alone with the television?

There was plenty of Scotch in the kitchen cabinet.

Perhaps he would dose himself, drink for as long as he could hold the bottle and then go into the darkness that way, asleep and oblivious. That was a nice dream, but it was more likely he would wake up just as everything was ending, just as he was suffocating and his body was bloated to the point of bursting because the atmospheric pressure had dropped to almost nothing.

God. They were going to die.

All of them.

People hurried past each other on the sidewalks; shop owners lowered grates over storefronts and locked their doors as if it were the end of any other day. He could see people sitting on porches as he drove, and a group of teens hurried through the crosswalk when he stopped at a red light two blocks from his destination. If a curfew had been imposed, they were likely trying to get home before a police car pulled up next to them.

At the next corner, he was held up by flashing lights and traffic cops in orange reflective vests. The National Guard had arrived to occupy the city. A massive convoy rolled through the light, its trucks banging and belching smoke as they pounded over grates and manhole covers and ground potholes into the asphalt. HUMVEEs mounted with large caliber machine guns and light armored vehicles strapped to flatbed trailers were interspersed throughout the mile-long string of troop carriers. Painted to blend with a desert landscape, the vehicles were foreign and threatening despite the American faces behind the wheels and more American faces that rode like cargo in the back of each. They brought no relief to the hundreds who watched them pass.

He went one more block and put on the left blinker when he reached the corner. The boy stirred in the back seat; neither of them said anything. When he turned, a cat darted out from between two parked cars, and he felt a glimmer of desire to run it down. It was gone as quickly as it had appeared, and he drove on, looking for a parking space at the end of the block.

When he found one, he pulled past it and backed in, getting as close to the curb as he could without scrubbing the tires. When they were in the space, he cut the engine and looked into the mirror.

The boy was watching him.

They looked at each other, then he smiled.

"Home at last," he said.

The boy said nothing.

The man looked away and put his finger on the radio button again.

No.

No. The radio was a way to stall; it wouldn't make this any easier. He drew his hand back and took the keys out of the ignition. Feeling the boy's eyes on him still, he opened his door and climbed out.

An air of unreality hung over the street. People walked past in quiet conversation; a bicycle passed him and the rider nodded hello even though he had no idea who the man was. There was unaccustomed civility all around him. This wasn't a dangerous neighborhood by any stretch of the imagination, but people here minded their own business. They kept their doors locked and put valuables out of sight when they parked their cars in the evening. He felt a palpable need to connect with these strangers, and he knew he was not alone.

He went to the back of the SUV and raised the hatch.

"It's time," he said, taking out the boy's small suitcase.

Wordless, the boy unsnapped his seatbelt and reached for the backpack on the seat beside him.

The man closed the tailgate and heard the passenger door open.

A cream-colored door opened on one of the row houses, and the woman stepped onto the small porch at the top of the walkway, a bright yellow bathrobe cinched around her body. A silhouette stood in the doorway behind her.

With the suitcase in one hand, he checked the back seat to make sure the boy had gathered all of his belongings. He had, and so the man shut the door and turned back to the walkway.

The boy took his hand.

The man braced himself and, together, they started up the path to the porch.

At the end of the walkway, just before they reached the steps, the boy paused.

The man looked down and met his eyes, then he forced himself to smile again. This was when he most needed to, for both their sakes, so he squeezed the boy's hand and gave him the look that said things were going to be okay.

The boy looked up the steps at his mother.

"H-hey, Mom," he said. And before she could respond, "Mom, I want Dad to sss-tay here. He can sleep in my room."

The man looked down at his son, dumbstruck.

The boy looked at him. "Rrr-onnie's a nice guy. He got to level ten on *Ghost Fighters*."

From the time he had awakened that morning, the man had not stopped wondering what he ought to say to his son. He had tried his best to protect the child from the catastrophe that was descending, to shield him from the fear if nothing else because no one would be spared the fury of the uncaring universe. Now, he was speechless because his son had asked them to do the simplest thing there was, the thing that at the same time was the most complicated and difficult he could imagine. The boy wanted them to abide each other: to be in one place, together, without anger.

He raised his eyes and looked at the woman.

She looked at him, looked at the boy, and then she turned to look silently at Ronnie who had come onto the porch to stand beside her.

"Ca-an he stay? Or else, can I go back with him?"

The boy labored over the words while he squeezed his father's hand.

The woman put out her own hand and said simply, "Let's go. It's almost time to get ready for bed. Are you hungry?"

The boy didn't move.

"M-m-my dad's gonna stay," he said looking into his mother's eyes. "Or else I'm leavin' too."

He took a backward step.

The woman's mouth fell open.

Her breath caught. Her eyes narrowed and she started toward them.

"*Boy if you...*"

"Wait a minute," the man said, raising his free hand as the boy scurried behind him.

Ronnie grabbed the woman's shoulders.

"Hold on," he said gently.

There was an instant of stillness. Then they heard the far-off peeps of a policeman's whistle and the deep-chested grunts of diesel engines turning onto their block.

The man turned around, knelt, and placed his hands on the boy's shoulders. Before he could speak, he heard Ronnie say, "Y'all come on in."

He looked over his shoulder and saw the woman disappear into the house. Ronnie stood beside the open door and waited.

He put his head back and sighed.

In the city, the Dark-Sky Scale was irrelevant. The abundant artificial light washed out the firmament and made star gazing impractical, if not impossible. Where they were now rated a Class 7.5, where Times Square itself was a Class

9. Above them was a dull expanse of matte gray with barely a handful of visible stars scattered across its breadth. In the unbounded stretch of drab sky, a much darker patch of utter blackness stood out like a coal sack, a creeping cloud of dark matter, a puncture in the very fabric of space.

He looked down at his son.

"Let's go inside," he said.

An hour later, they had eaten a light meal, and the boy was submerged in the bathtub. Half-hidden by mountains of bubbles and surrounded by a naval armada, he babbled and fired imaginary torpedoes at a plastic missile cruiser while his mother sat on the toilet seat watching and listening.

Out back on the tiny patio, the two men sat on wrought iron chairs and watched the sky. An open bottle of Chivas Regal rested on the concrete between them. The blinking lights of passenger jets flickered overhead, some climbing away to nothingness, others gliding toward the airport out beyond the suburbs. The man gazed at the far-away hole in the heavens and listened to cats scavenging in the garbage cans beyond the garden fence. As he watched the patch of darkness, it began to rotate. Its movement was slow at first, hardly noticeable, but it was there. It was happening.

He thought about his son, and he hoped the boy would sleep well that night.

Milton Keynes UK
Ingram Content Group UK Ltd.
UKHW030718051124
450766UK00001B/34